Arben's Vent

GORDON AMICK

319 press

Published by 319 Press LLC

P.O. Box 341117
Austin, Tx 78734
www.319press.com

ISBN - 979-8-9908959-3-5 (ebook)
ISBN - 979-8-9908959-4-2 (Paperback)
ISBN - 979-8-9908959-5-9 (Hardcover)

Gordon Amick | gordonamick.com

Cover design by Flamingo Studios

To John Jackson. You are missed.

One

Tarrant County Mental Health Services Center

Tuesday 8:00 am

Arben Davis, a nineteen-year-old, was escorted down a stark and lengthy corridor by Tyrell, a patient care assistant at Tarrant County Mental Health Services Center. They were headed to Dr. Andrews' office where Arben, having just arrived, would undergo a routine examination, a standard procedure for all new patients.

The sterile, dreary environment, with its bare walls and tiled floors, amplified Arben's anxiety. He walked cautiously beside Tyrell, then suddenly turned to his left as he heard the distant cries of men and women in distress. The sounds were deeply unsettling—screams, gibberish, and bizarre noises echoed through the halls. Though Arben was frightened, he took some solace in knowing they were too far away to pose any real threat. Still, the unsettling chorus heightened his concern as he continued walking with Tyrell.

As they traveled down the desolate hallway, Arben suddenly turned sharply to his right, startled by voices that sounded familiar—like the ones he had been hearing since childhood in his backyard.

He looked around when he heard a familiar voice say, "Caaaaarrrrr! Reeeeeaaaaallll!" The voice wasn't coming from the same place as the screams and grunts. It seemed to be originating from the opposite direction but much closer.

Startled and confused by their nonsensical message, Arben looked left then right, his anxiety mounting. The disjointed voice added to the chaos in his mind, making the experience even more overwhelming.

Additional invisible voices joined in, chanting, "Me. Me. Me. Top. Top. Top. Me. Me. Me."

Arben furrowed his brow and slowed down, trying to listen more closely. "Who is that?" he asked, his voice tinged with curiosity and apprehension.

Tyrell glanced toward the patient ward, nonchalantly replying, "Oh, that's just some folks complainin'. No worries."

With a slight tug, Tyrell gently encouraged Arben to keep moving, trying to resume the pace and ease his concerns.

Arben shook his head and pointed in the opposite direction. "Those."

Tyrell turned to listen. "I don't hear nothin' from over there."

Arben mumbled, "No one ever does," disappointment clear in his voice.

"How's that?" Tyrell asked.

Arben didn't respond as the voices continued filling his mind, their collective murmur growing louder and more echoey. He could hear them clearly, even though Tryell and others could not. This isolation in his perception only added to his sense of confusion and anxiety.

"Caaaaarrrrr! Me. Me. Me. Top. Top. Top. Reeeeaaaalllll! Top. Top. Top. Me. Me. Me."

"Stop!" Arben shouted, his voice reverberating down the hall.

Tyrell halted, concern etched on his face. "What's wrong?"

"Too many people talking," Arben said, overwhelmed by the cacophony of voices only he could hear.

The unfazed orderly gripped Arben's arm tightly, urging him swiftly down down the hall. Arben complied without resistance, but as they passed the break room next to the doctor's office, a low hum caught his attention. The sound rapidly increased in intensity, prompting Arben to halt and instinctively retreat. However, Tyrell maintained his tight grip on Arben's arm.

Arben twisted and turned, desperately seeking a position where the low hum wasn't resonating so painfully in his head. As the noise reached an unbearable level, Arben tightly covered his ears with his hands, trying to block out the sound.

Tyrell led Arben into the office of clinical psychiatrist Dr. Stanislaus Andrews. In his early forties, Dr. Andrews wore slacks, a button-down shirt, and tie, with his lab coat draped over the back of his desk chair. His office was cluttered with books and files, while the walls were adorned with diplomas, certifications, and artwork.

Arben kept his hands tightly over his ears, attempting to block out the overwhelming noise and voices as Tyrell guided him to a chair across from Dr. Andrews' desk. The doctor, displaying a mix of calm professionalism and genuine concern, looked up from Arben's file. "What's going on?"

Tyrell replied, "Arben Davis is on a three-day voluntary hold. He was fine in the lobby, but he started complainin' about too many people talkin'. I think he was hearin' the other residents. He put his hands over his ears while we was walkin' over here."

Seated in the chair, Arben continued twisting and turning, trying to alleviate the noise rumbling in his head. Desperately, he reached into his pocket where he'd always kept cotton balls for stuffing in his ears, but they were missing. Panic set in, and he bolted for the door. Tyrell swiftly blocked his path, leaving Arben feeling trapped and increasingly desperate.

Arben gave the doctor a pleading look, his face tight with agony. "It's loud," he cried.

"Tell me what you're hearing," Dr. Andrews urged, his tone calm and reassuring.

"It's loud!" Arben repeated, turning his head left and right, unable to escape the worsening throbbing pain. "A loud hum. Voices. Lots of them. My head! Ahhh! Make it stop. I need cotton balls."

The doctor calmly stepped across the room, unlocked a cabinet drawer, and retrieved a syringe. "Mr. Davis, it's okay. We're gonna help you."

Frantic and desperate, Arben started pacing around the room, twisting and turning. "Please, make it stop!" he cried out, his voice filled with agony.

Dr. Andrews nodded at Tyrell, who immediately wrapped his

arms around Arben in a bear hug to restrain him. With practiced precision, the doctor administered the shot.

"This will help you relax," the doctor said as he emptied the syringe into Arben's arm.

Despite the unbearable pain in his head, the sudden ambush and injection shocked Arben. He immediately began squirming, trying to free himself. "Stop!" he shouted.

Tyrell held a tight grip on Arben, keeping him from hurting himself or the doctor. "It's okay, Arben," Dr. Andrews reassured him. "You're going to start feeling tired. Try to relax. Don't fight it."

Arben felt a warm wave wash through his body as he quickly lost his ability to resist. Tyrell sat him in a chair and stood nearby to keep Arben from falling as he went limp.

After Arben was relocated to a private room, Dr. Andrews returned to his desk to continue reading Arben's history: *Arben Davis, nineteen years old, professional musician, pianist, admitted for a three-day voluntary commitment after a recent suicide attempt. Parent's deceased. History of odd behavior but no formal diagnosis of cognitive disorder.*

Dr. Andrews flipped through the file and pulled out the report submitted by the hospital, documenting their findings after Arben was admitted and treated for an attempted suicide.

Two

Arben's childhood home, Austin, Texas

20 years earlier

Twenty-eight-year-old Benny Davis, a petty drug dealer and aspiring rockstar, stood in the den of the dilapidated rent house he shared with Arlene, his common-law wife.

The room was adorned with concert posters affixed to the walls with thumb tacks and tape, velvet paintings in plastic frames, and enlarged photos of Benny performing with his band; the background blurred to hide the reality that the room was nearly empty of fans.

Wearing bell bottom jeans, a dashiki, a leather necklace, headband and wristband, along with an electric guitar slung around his neck, Benny slammed the strings of the guitar, blasting an out-of-tune chord that reverberated throughout the entire house and beyond. He followed this with a long, ear-piercing note that sent the neighborhood dogs howling. While sustaining the deafening note, Benny spun around with his eyes closed then threw his right arm in the air, striking the classic rock star's pose. He completed the sequence striking a loud, final chord, closing his eyes again as everything inside the house shook and rattled.

Nineteen-year-old Arlene Davis sauntered in with a cigarette in one hand and a pregnancy test in the other. As an occasional waitress, she contributed to the household finances, but her primary role until that day had been to support her husband's delusions of being a rock star.

She tapped Benny on the shoulder, interrupting his guitar practice.

"Baby, what the hell?" Benny remarked, clearly annoyed by the intrusion. "Did you hear that sustain?" His droopy-eyed expression revealed his intoxication. "Man, it was freakin' astral."

Arlene thrust the pregnancy test in front of his face, forcing him to look at it.

"What's that?" he asked.

"It's a salad fork," she quipped. "What the hell you think it is?"

"Tell me you ain't pregnant."

Arlene grinned and blew a plume of cigarette smoke.

"Dammit, baby. That ain't cool. The band's about to book some serious travel dates. Get rid of it."

She gasped. "I can't believe you said that. 'Sides, I ain't in the band." Taking another drag from her cigarette, she nonchalantly added, "So, we'll have us a kid. It ain't no big deal?"

Benny swung his guitar behind him, crouched down and retrieved a bag of pills from the guitar case. He popped a pill into his mouth and washed it down with a swallow of beer. "No, baby. It ain't cool."

"Gimme a Xanex," she said, grabbing his beer and taking a sip.

"You can't party if you're pregnant."

She scoffed. "I ain't been pregnant long enough for it to matter. 'Sides, it's just Xanex."

"Baby, we don't need a kid."

"It ain't up to us," she said, chasing the pill down with a big chug of beer. "It's what God wanted for us."

"It ain't God. It's 'cause you screwed up."

"*I* screwed up? You was there too."

"You said you was on the pill."

"I am, but the pill don't always work. 'Specially when God wants us to have a baby. Aren't you excited? He'll have your good looks and my smarts. He'll be our perfect little angel, sent from God. It's meant to be."

Benny shook his head. "We're *meant* to be rockin' out on world tour, not gettin' tied down by some kid."

Three

Tarrant County Mental Health Services Center

Tuesday 8:30 am

Dr. Andrews read through the hospital's findings on Arben's suicide attempt, but the report only posed more questions than answers. He delved deeper, quickly becoming engrossed in Arben's file, intrigued by the details and curious about what had caused his unusual outburst earlier that required him to be sedated. The case seemed fascinating, and he was ready to dig deeper when the hospital administrator, Dr. Jason Campos appeared in the doorway, casting a shadow over the room.

"Doctor, I need you to supervise the new hire on rounds today and tomorrow."

Dr. Andrews shook his head. "Sir, I already have a full plate, and I'm just beginning my assessment of the new admit, Arben Davis."

"I'm sorry Stan. Change of plans. Drs. Cruz and Hoffman

will be doing the assessment of Mr. Davis. You'll be doing the background."

"What do you mean *background?* Dr. Cruz is taking the lead on the Mental Status Exam (MSE), which we all update independently, but as far as background, we always do our own patient research, as needed."

"Yes, well, I've instituted a new procedure for all new intakes. One doctor will do a complete background investigation while the other two conduct the hands-on evaluation. Given Mr. Davis's complicated history, with at least one suicide attempt, possibly more, I believe you are best suited for the background."

"Sir—"

"Doctor," Campos interrupted. "I suspect Mr. Davis will be with us for an extended period, so you will have plenty of opportunities to interact with him."

"At this point, I'd rather make sure we arrive at the proper diagnosis."

"Of course. But we both know that takes time."

Dr. Andrews gave the director a suspicious look, sensing a prelude to something. "And?"

"And that makes the background information all the more crucial. Public scrutiny of this and all facilities statewide have been increasing, so we have to cross all T's and dot all I's."

"Respectfully, sir, I am a highly trained therapists with over ten years of experience. I am *not* an administrator."

"I'm sorry Stan. The decision's been made. Of course you're an outstanding therapist, but you're also the most thorough when it comes to background and documentation."

Dr. Andrews tightened his lips and shook his head.

Dr. Campos continued, "I want you to interview everyone who may have relevant information about Mr. Davis and add their information to his file."

Defiantly, Dr. Andrews replied, "I understand, but I'm still going to talk with Mr. Davis, at length, I might add, before I submit my report."

"Fine. As long as you have the report on my desk before Friday morning."

Four

Tarrant County Mental Health Services Center

Tuesday 9:00 am

After Dr. Campos left, Dr Andrews immediately began reworking his schedule to make room for a full assessment of Arben. It would be a few days before he could sit down with the young man, but Dr. Andrews was determined to remain involved in the process and committed to arriving at the right diagnosis.

He glanced at his watch and noted that he had less than thirty minutes before he was expected in the patient ward to supervise rounds.

For most patients, background information was gathered from immediate family members and close friends. Arben's case presented several difficulties, with both of his parents deceased and having no siblings or close friends.

Dr. Andrews flipped through the case file and extracted a short list of people who had interacted with Arben that might have relevant information about his upbringing and recent experiences. Some, like the ER doctor and staff psychologist had already provided their observations. The rest would require a few phone calls.

- Dr. V.M. Rice - ER doc treating suicide, report attached.
- Dr. Enrique Navarro – Hospital staff psychologist, report attached.
- Marianne Railey – Piano instructor, 10-year relationship with patient, teacher, friend. CONTACT.
- Tova Rawlins – Signatory for commitment to TCMHSC, Unknown relationship, possible professional connection. CONTACT.

With his remaining time, Dr. Andrews read through the summary reports from Arben's ER admission after an attempted suicide:

Mr. Davis arrived via ambulance after near drowning. Aspirated lungs, minimal fluids. Patient despondent and non-verbal throughout initial exam. Medical history incomplete. Numerous healed scars consistent with childhood trauma. Parents deceased. Administered standard medications along with antidepressant. Psych consult ordered. -Dr. Weldon Rice, MD, BCEM, ABEM.

Dr. Andrews extracted several key points for his notes: *Deceased parents, abused child, depression, suicide attempt(s).* It was a pattern he had seen before.

He then proceeded to Dr. Navarro's psychological assessment, eager to gain insight into Arben's current mental state and history.

Patient lethargic and detached, likely from medications but able to converse. Severely depressed. Refused to discuss suicide attempt. Generally calm with exception of periodic outburst (blows to concrete wall) triggered by the mention of mother's recent death. Patient blames himself for mother's overdose. Cited "God punishes evil thoughts." Indications of childhood abuse both physical and emotional. Expressed substantial guilt over both parent's deaths. Indications of delusional ideation, demonstrated by stated belief that he is responsible for parents and other family members' deaths. Possible dissociative disorder from psychological trauma. Patient not deemed an immediate danger but signs of schizotypal personality disorder evidenced by admission of hearing voices. Voices are most concerning. Recommend 3-day voluntary commitment at an In-Patient facility for in-depth assessment. Recommend mandatory if voluntary refused. Dr. Enrico Navarro, PsyD. LPC-S.

After updating his notes, Dr Andrews remained at his desk pondering what he had just read and formulating a plan for completing the background report.

Abused, neglected, professional musician? Dr. Andrews thought, wondering if Arben was simply a mistreated or misunderstood creative type. He noted the address of Arben's childhood home along with some information listed on his intake form. *Raised in a rough part of East Austin, father a musician and convicted drug dealer, mother's death likely from overdose.* He paused to consider a few possible conclusions. *Addicts. One parent is bad,* he thought. *Both can leave a child in a hopeless situation.*

He closed the file and headed out the door, his mind still processing everything he had learned about Arben Davis.

Five

Tarrant County Mental Health Services Center

Tuesday 11:30 am

Three hours after being sedated, Arben lay sleeping in a private room.

Dr. Joanna Cruz, a 32-year-old staff psychiatrist, sat in a chair beside the bed. The attractive young woman wore a lab coat over her hospital scrubs, and her long hair was pulled into a ponytail. Dr. Cruz always maintained a professional appearance and demeanor, but her soft voice and green eyes gave her a disarming quality that helped put patients at ease.

Sitting in the chair with her head down, reviewing Arben's file on her electronic tablet, Dr. Cruz looked up when Arben stirred. Slowly, he opened his eyes and stared at her.

"Welcome back, Arben. I'm Dr. Cruz. You can call me Joanna."

Arben remained still, glancing around the stark room. The

pale green walls gave the place a sterile feel. A small window ushered in the poor light from a dim, overcast sky. He peered over the rails of the hospital bed, noting a small desk with a lamp nearby. The florescent light overhead was off, so apart from the window, the room was dimly lit by the desk lamp, enhancing the sense of isolation in the space.

Leaning against the closed door stood Tyrell, the same man who had escorted Arben to Dr. Andrews' office and restrained him while the doctor sedated him. Arben rubbed the injection site, glaring at Tyrell.

His eyes returned to Dr. Cruz as he lay still on his back. Though disoriented, Arben had no trouble expressing his sole thought, "I want to go home." His voice was tinged with both confusion and longing.

The doctor gave a pleasant grin, her bright eyes capturing Arben's attention.

"I understand, Arben," she said gently. "But for now, we need to make sure you're safe and well. Tyrell is going to escort you to an exam room for a short physical exam. Okay?"

Arben remained expressionless as he gave a slight nod.

"Great," the doctor said, rising to her feet. "I'll see you in a few minutes."

She turned her attention to her phone, tapping and swiping as she started for the door. Meanwhile, Tyrell moved closer to help Arben up from the bed.

As soon as Dr. Cruz opened the door, Arben sat bolt upright and covered his ears.

"It's loud," Arben said, hearing the same loud noise he heard when he arrived earlier that morning.

Dr. Cruz, preoccupied with her phone, disregarded Arben's remark as she continued away from the room.

Arben kept his hands over his ears as Tyrell took him by the arm and guided him toward the door. He grimaced, clamping his hands tighter over his ears as he tried to back away. Twisting and turning, he desperately sought a position where the sound was manageable, but the pain continued to grow until it was unbearable. With a sudden burst of energy, he twisted and jerked himself free from Tyrell's grip, backing into the corner farthest from the door.

"C'mon man," Tyrell grumbled, clearly frustrated by Arben's resistance. He grabbed Arben's arm and attempted to pull him toward the door.

Forced to uncover his ears, Arben grabbed the door frame and fought to stay in his room. "No!" he shouted. "It's too loud. Stop. Please!"

Tyrell realized his strength might injure Arben if he forced him out the door, so he released his grip and allowed Arben to remain in his room.

Dr. Cruz looked up from her phone, noticing the commotion. She hurried down the hall and stood in the doorway, seeing Arben pressed into the corner with his hands over his ears. His distress was obvious.

"What's going on?" Dr. Cuz asked, concern evident in her voice.

"It's loud," Arben replied.

She stepped in the room and closed the door behind her. Arben glanced at the closed door before slowly and cautiously pulling his hands away from his ears. He carefully turned his head from side to side. The offending sound was still present, but it was no longer painful.

Dr. Cruz reflected on Arben's strange behavior with curiosity and concern. He had gone from calm to highly agitated and back to calm in a matter of a seconds. She remained guarded, as she had seen patients become dangerously violent with little or no warning, and this was Arben's second episode in less than four hours.

"Is it better now?" she asked, keeping herself between Arben and the door.

Arben stared at Dr. Cruz, fearing she might give him shot like Dr. Andrews had or force him into the hallway where the noise produced excruciating pain. He said nothing, maintaining a suspicious eye on her as he shifted over to the bed and positioned himself as far from the door as possible. The pain had passed, but the concern on his face remained.

"It's okay," Dr. Cruz said, responding to the fear on Arben's face. Noting that his hands were at his side and no longer covering his ears, she continued, "Can I assume the loud noise has stopped?"

Arben gave no response.

The doctor waited through a long silence while both stared at one another. "Is it only loud in the hallway and not in the room?"

Arben hesitated, then gave a slight, single nod. The noise had been overwhelming in the hallway, but with the door closed it was bearable.

He studied the doctor carefully. His trust in the doctors and staff was fragile at best. In the last few hours, he had been locked up in a strange place, given a shot that felt more like an assault, and manhandled into the hallway despite clearly expressing his pain. He was rightfully leery.

Through a skeptical squint, he again offered only a slight nod.

Dr. Cruz took a seat in the only chair in the room. She opened her tablet and quickly scanned Dr. Andrews' details of the incident in his office earlier that morning, hoping to better understand Arben's current state of distress. Sedating him was an option, but she chose to employ empathy and patience.

"Out in the hallway," Dr. Cruz began, "do you hear the same loud noise you heard this morning outside the doctor's offices?"

Arben stared blankly at the doctor, suspicion in his eyes as he considered the question. Along with his distrust of the doctor and the institution, memories of countless failed conversations about his hearing issues flashed through his mind. Too many times he'd been greeted with skepticism and dismissal, which only deepened his wariness now.

You won't understand, he thought. *No one does*. He shrugged and appeared indifferent, deciding not to talk about it.

"Listen," Dr. Cruz said in her sweet, peaceful tone. "If we work together, maybe we can find a way to fix what's going on with you."

Arben grimaced. *Fixed* was a word that triggered more bad memories. He had asked countless doctors to fix his hearing but was always told his *exceptional hearing* didn't need fixing. Each hopeful visit to a doctor ended with the same disappointing outcome. He'd given up long ago on being *fixed*, and the mere mention of that word irritated him.

The doctor stood up and said, "Arben, we need to perform a

quick intake exam. Normally we do that in an exam room, but we can do it here. I'll be right back." She exited the room and returned a few minutes later with an assistant, pushing a cart.

Six

Tarrant County Mental Health Services Center

Tuesday 11:45 am

The moment Dr. Cruz entered Arben's room, followed by Nurse Vanessa with a cart full of medical equipment, supplies, and a computer, Arben instinctively retreated to the corner. His eyes fixed on the hypodermic needle among the instruments.

"It's okay, Arben," Dr. Cruz reassured, extending a calming hand.

His gaze remained locked on the needle, fear etched across his face.

"We're just going to do a simple exam, mostly talking," the doctor explained.

With a gentle demeanor, the nurse approached Arben with a blood pressure cuff. "I assure you this won't hurt," she said softly. "Why don't you take a seat on the bed."

Still wary but familiar with the blood pressure cuff, he

reluctantly settled onto the bed.

The nurse carefully wrapped the device around his arm and began to inflate it.

As Vanessa conducted the physical exam—checking blood pressure, temperature, weight, and height—Dr. Cruz began the standard observational assessment. She opened her electronic tablet and started running through the MSE checklist.

She started with Arben's appearance, noting his grooming was clean and neat, with his hair cut short and brushed. He was dressed casually in jeans and a button-up shirt. No body odor or unhygienic characteristics were observed.

"Can you stand," Dr. Cruz asked Arben. He complied, and she noted his stability and absence of any visible signs of tremors or balance issues.

The nurse updated the records on the computer, recording Arben measurements: five foot ten inches, one hundred-forty pounds. Heart rate of seventy-two and blood pressure of 130/84.

Dr. Cruz added her observations to the file, remarking on Arben thin build and slight slouch, indicating a lack of confidence.

Demeanor: *suspicious and guarded, almost defensive yet cooperative. Limited eye contact and minimal facial expression. Slight foot tapping suggests nervousness but no observable psychomotor activity.* ***Impulse control:*** *unremarkable with no abnormal movement, but obvious tension.* ***Speech:*** *limited and slightly monosyllabic but clear and fluent.*

After the nurse finished recording Arben's vitals and basic information, she retrieved the nylon tourniquet and hypodermic needle from the tray.

Arben jumped up from the bed and backed into the corner. "I don't want that," he declared.

The nurse refrained from approaching Arben, allowing Dr. Cruz to defuse the situation.

Dr. Cruz stood a few feet back from Arben, not wanting him to feel crowded or intimidated. "Arben," she said. "It's okay. She's not going to give you a shot. She's just needs to draw some blood. You might feel a very slight prick, but that's it."

Arben furrowed his brow, reluctant to trust someone with a needle. He studied the bright, inviting expressions on both ladies' faces and slowly nodded.

The nurse motioned for him to take a seat on the bed. "I promise this won't take long, and like the doctor said, you'll only feel a quick stick." She slipped the rubber band around his arm while maintaining a cheery voice. "See? We're almost done." She pulled the cap off the needle, causing Arben to wince. "It's okay," she reassured, gently stroking his arm before tucking it under her arm so he wouldn't move. Being very skilled, the nurse slipped the needle in quickly while keeping Arben's attention focused on her. "You're past the worst part," she said, making eye contact with him for a moment before pulling the first vile out of the unit and slipping a second one in. "Okay," she said with a lilt as she extracted the needle from his arm. "Done. That's wasn't so bad."

Arben gave a slight smile and said, "Okay."

Vanessa secured a bandage on the puncture mark and smiled at Arben. "You did great." She marked the vials and set them on the tray next to the computer.

Dr. Cruz resumed her assessment, making notes on her tablet

while Arben sat silently on the bed.

Mood: *sullen or depressed. Triggered by hypodermic. Affect incongruent.*

She glanced at the remaining sections of the form—thought, perception, cognition, and judgment—and made a mental note to complete them during her upcoming interview with Arben.

The nurse organized all the items on the rolling cart and headed for the door. However, Dr. Cruz reached out and stopped her before she opened it.

"Go quickly," Dr. Cruz instructed the nurse.

As Arben saw the doctor reach for the doorknob, he quickly covered his ears.

The nurse hurried out of the room, and Dr. Cruz swiftly closed the door. She turned to Arben. "You okay?"

He cautiously turned his head from side to side as he slowly pulled his hands from his ears and nodded.

"Great," Dr. Cruz said, swiping through her tablet to a blank screen where she could make notes.

"You grew up in Austin, graduated high school, and now you're a professional musician; apparently a very good one," she said with a hint of admiration.

Arben gave a slight nod.

"Do you remember when you started playing?"

Arben felt determined to remain obstinate, as he had low expectations for any doctor claiming to *help* him. However, he remembered what Tova—his friend, manager, and the person who convinced him to be committed to the facility—had said: *You need to talk to someone about what happened. And the sooner you talk to them, the sooner you and I can get back out on the road.*

Sensing Arben's internal struggle, Dr. Cruz waited patiently. She hoped her genuine curiosity and gentle mannerisms would make him feel more comfortable and thus more forthcoming. "Do you remember when you started playing?" she repeated softly.

With Tova's words in mind, Arben lowered his guard and said, "Ms. Railey taught me."

Dr. Cruz noticed the slight shift in Arben's posture. "How old you were when you started taking lessons?"

Arben thought about one of the best days of his life: the day he met his only other friend besides Tova, his piano teacher, Marianne Railey. The memory brought the first smile to his face since arriving at TCMHSC.

"Five or six," he replied, his smile lingering. "It was the first time I played a grand piano. Ms. Railey played a middle C and I said 'C.'" His smile grew. "She said 'I'm impressed you know the notes.'"

Dr. Cruz's expression matched Arben's growing smile. "How did you already know the notes? Wasn't it your first lesson?"

"Dad taught me the notes."

His bright expression waned slightly as he relived the bittersweet beginning of his love of music.

Seven

Arben's childhood home, Austin, Texas

16 years earlier

From a very young age, Arben was captivated by music. Once he learned to stand, he would position himself in front of the old rickety piano in the den and reach up to strike the keys. Despite the piano being far out of tune, the sound always brought a smile to his face. He loved letting the notes ring out as long as possible. Although, he often cried at the sound of Benny's guitar—usually due to the extreme volume—by age four, his love of music was unquestionable.

One day, Benny was sitting at the old piano, picking out a melody for a new song when Arben appeared and reached up to strike a few notes.

"Here, little man," Benny said, lifting Arben and setting him on the bench next to him. At first, Arben was apprehensive, feeling intimidated by his father's sudden interest in him. Until then, all

Arben had experienced was a distant father who spoke to him only him when necessary: "Stop crying." "Are you hungry?" "Need to potty?"

Bright eyed, Arben looked at his father then down at the keys. He played a single note and glanced at his father.

"That's F-sharp," Benny said.

"Huh," Arben grunted, tilting his head inquisitively.

"F-sharp. That's a F-sharp," Benny repeated, louder.

Arben struck a different note.

"That's A."

Arben smiled and hit the first note again.

"That's F-sharp again."

Arben giggled and hit another note.

"That's C-sharp. You're rockin' little man. That's a F-sharp chord."

Arben continued picking out notes, a smile on his face as his fingers dancing across the keys.

Benny stood, leaving Arben seated at the piano. "Baby," Benny called out to his wife while strolling across the room. "Where's my bag a picks? I ran out last night throwin' 'em to the crowd." Although he neglected to mention that the *crowd* was less than forty people.

The entire encounter between Arben and his father lasted less than five minutes, but even after Benny walked away, the joy of discovering music and the brief moment of connection with his father left a lasting impression on young Arben.

Arben remained at the piano, tinkering and enjoying the resonance and impression each note left. He giggled every time he struck three notes that formed a chord. He figured out three-note chords repeatedly, thoroughly entertaining himself. Each time he discovered a new combination that thrilled him, he'd look at his parents, hoping they would recognize his accomplishment and share his excitement, but they never noticed.

He soon learned how to climb onto the piano bench by himself, but his reach only extended to a limited number of keys in either direction. To overcome this limitation, he would climb down and slide the bench to the left or right, enabling him to reach the higher or lower notes.

Having slid the bench to the left, he resumed playing, striking one, two and three notes together to form chords. He'd been enjoying himself until he hit the lowest G on the piano.

Suddenly, he felt a sharp pulse cut through his head, like a shock. He winced at the unpleasant sensation. Disturbed and confused, he looked at his parents for comfort or reassurance, but they were oblivious to his distress. He stared at the piano and struck the same low G again, experiencing the same result. The shock was startling, causing him to pivot his head. The instrument that had brought him such joy now seemed to bite him, leaving him suspicious and irritated.

He stuck his finger in one ear and cautiously struck a few higher notes, letting them ring out. Avoiding the lowest notes, he tried a few others, and having eliminated the shock, smiled and continued playing. He returned to his usual routine: striking a pleasing combination of notes and glancing at his parents for approval. Their lack of interest never wavered. However, Benny and Arlene's indifference didn't deter Arben from spending hours at the piano, as his love for music remained undiminished.

Those early experiences fueled Arben's passion for music, setting the stage for his future as an accomplished musician.

Eight

Tarrant County Mental Health Services Center

Tuesday noon

D*ad taught me the notes.* Arbens words replayed in Dr. Cruz's thoughts as she noted the change in Arben's demeanor when his father was mentioned. *Unresolved issues? Sadness over loss or bad memories from childhood?*

Dr. Cruz felt a pang of empathy as she considered the possible weight of Arben's past. She took a moment to update the MSE.

Thoughts: *stream of thought normal with occasional mutism, file indicates auditory hallucinations but none observed.* ***Cognition:*** *normal.* ***Insight/Judgement:*** *fair to good, possible distortion of childhood.*

"So, your father taught you to play the piano before Marianne Railey?" Dr. Cruz asked, resuming her assessment.

Arben gave Dr. Cruz an odd look before correcting her. "Ms. Railey."

"Sorry. Ms. Railey. But she took over your piano lessons after your father started?"

Arben's expression tightened as he recalled how Benny had shown him the notes on the piano and nothing more. He never offered any meaningful teaching or instruction, nor did he ever express any interest in Arben's musical talent or career.

"No," Arben said after a pause. "Ms. Railey taught me to read music. She said if you learn to read music you can play anything you want."

"So, I assume you can play anything you want?"

Arben nodded, a humble smile spreading across his face.

"Maybe you can play for us once we get you fixed up," she suggested.

"Okay," he said with a smirk, again irked by her using the word *fixed.*

"You were playing the piano last Saturday night before you jumped into Lake Austin."

The memory of that day sent a wash of guilt through Arben. He pressed his lips together, showing reluctance to discuss it.

Dr. Cruz had often dealt with patients who avoided painful memories, but she hoped that talking might ease Arben's burden. "Do you remember what happened?" she gently asked, trying to encourage him to open up without pressing too hard.

Arben's jaw tightened as he looked away, struggling to push aside the memory of the day he jumped in the lake, ending his career.

"It doesn't matter," he said with an angry tone of indifference.

Arben's sharp tone and tense body language signaled to Dr.

Cruz that she needed to reconsider her approach. Otherwise, there was a risk he might shut down completely or react unpredictably, which would derail the interview.

Dr. Cruz restored her disarming smile and pleasant tone. “Let’s go back to when you first started playing. Tell me about those first performances. I bet it was exciting.”

Her words helped Arben bury his dark thoughts of jumping in the lake and focus on his two favorite things: playing the piano and performing live.

Throughout most of Arben’s school career, he felt like an outsider. He was bullied and ridiculed, often for no other reason than he was different. That all changed during his sophomore year when he decided to enter the school talent show.

As he took the stage, the unruly crowd cackled and booed, unnerving Arben to the point he nearly ran away. Determined to prove them wrong and redeem himself for all those years of abuse, he forced himself to sit at the piano. Blocking out all the noise, he launched into an impressive rendition of Libertango, a high-energy Argentinian tango. Within seconds, the crowd went silent, completely captivated. When he finished, they erupted in a raucous applause. As he walked off stage, he was greeted with backslaps, high-fives, and congratulations. Arben felt a recognition that he had never thought possible.

As he recalled the memory, a smile spread across his face. His expression and disposition lightened, becoming more open and accommodating.

“The talent show,” Arben said. “I showed ’em.”

“You showed them you were a talented?”

Arben nodded, his smile widening. "They loved me. It was fun, like in the videos."

"You watch other pianists on YouTube?"

"And symphonies," he added.

"Yes. I watch stuff on YouTube too," she said, matching his smile. "What a great memory. Thank you for sharing that." She made a few quick notes then continued, "Tell me, when you first started performing, did you have problems with voices or loud noises?"

He still wasn't ready to talk about his deeper issues, but with his defenses down, he let his thoughts spilled out.

"The applause was loud."

"When you performed at the high school talent show?"

He nodded proudly.

Dr. Cruz noted his pride and the significance of that moment in his life. "And they loved you," Dr. Cruz deliberately parroted, aiming to make him smile and strengthen the rapport they were building. "Did you win?"

"Second."

"Wow, congratulations. You must have been popular after that."

The smile on Arben's face continued but began to fade as the doctor's remark about popularity led his thoughts to the aftermath of the talent show.

Memories of the high praise and congratulations Arben received after performing Libertango gave way to the stark realities of the days and weeks following the event when life returned to normal. Occasionally, he'd receive *some* recognition while wandering the hallways of school—a few high-fives, and the occasional "hey piano dude"—but Arben felt the painful return to being an outsider. There were no party invitations, no friendly conversation, and no real acknowledgment beyond passing nods.

Arben's recollection of that event brought up other memories, reinforcing his belief that, despite being briefly accepted by the masses at the talent show, he would always be an outsider.

He looked at the doctor, shrugged, and somberly said, "They still didn't like me. They never did."

"Now, I know that's not true," Dr. Cruz responded patronizingly. "But I tell you what. Why don't we break for lunch? You can relax for a while, and I'll see you in an hour."

After she left, Arben stretched out on the bed and withdrew into more disheartening memories from his school days.

Nine

Overton Elementary School, Austin, Texas

13 years earlier

First grade brings new experiences for all children, but for Arben, the excitement came with several unique challenges. Just days into the school year, Arben was troubled by a low hum in writing class that only he heard. The sound seemed to originate from a utility closet next to the classroom. The first time he heard it, class was about to begin. Arben moved to a seat far from the door, hoping to escape the noise. However, Mr. Modawell, the seasoned teacher who had seen it all in the inner-city school system, objected. "Mr. Davis," he said firmly. "I assigned you a seat. Please return to it."

"I hear a noise when I sit there."

The teacher, known for his lack of tolerance for what he considered nonsense, responded saying, "Mr. Davis, please return to your assigned seat."

Arben complied, but as he sat, he covered his ears, blocking out the offending sound along with the teacher's voice. It wasn't long before Mr. Modawell called on him.

"Huh?" Arben responded.

"Mr. Davis," the teacher said, motioning for Arben to uncover his ears. Arben pulled his hand away from one ear. "Please uncover your ears and listen to what I am saying."

"I can't. The noise bothers me."

Several students snickered.

"Would you prefer going to the principal's office?" Mr. Modawell asked sternly.

Arben, not understanding what being sent to the principal's office meant, shook his head. "That's too far away to hear."

The teacher's face hardened, clearly not amused by Arben's response. Several students laughed, and the intolerant teacher swiftly whipped a referral form from his desk and began filling it out. He motioned for Arben to approach and handed him the paper. "Since you insist on disrupting my class, I am sending you to the principal's office."

Arben explained the situation to the principal, asserting that he had heard a loud noise. Consequently, the principal decided to send him to the school nurse.

The school nurse conducted several basic hearing tests on Arben. Afterward, she remarked, "Arben, you have exceptional hearing. Your problem is that your ears are far more sensitive than most." She filled out the evaluation form and added, "I'm going to recommend that your parents take you to a hearing specialist."

Arben nodded, but felt a tinge of disappointment. He had

hoped the nurse would discover something that would silence the distracting hum he had heard in class. *Exceptional hearing*, he thought. *That's why nobody hears what I hear.* While the explanation offered *some* relief, it also confirmed that he was *different*—a word he immediately disliked. With no friends, he longed to fit in, to be like everyone else, and not stand apart as different.

Noticing Arben's sullen expression, the nurse offered, "I'll talk with your teacher about changing your seat."

Mr. Modawell allowed Arben to switch seats, but this special treatment only made Arben more of a target. Some students kicked his desk as they passed by, while others waited for the teacher to look away before knocking his supplies to the floor. Arben grew more and more frustrated, expecting Mr. Modawell to step in. When it became clear no one would come to his aid, he decided to take matters into his own hands.

At first, Arben tried to defend himself by keeping his hands over his supplies whenever someone walked past. However, the effort proved distracting, and the students quickly turned his reaction into a game. Some would lunge toward him just to watch him flinch, laughing at his overreactions. His constant scrambling to protect his belongings drew smirks, snickers, and outright laughter—not just from tormentors, but also from others who couldn't help but join in the cruel amusement.

His anger and frustration grew until, one day, he'd had enough. A less-intimidating kid sauntered by and deliberately knocked Arben's books to the floor. In an instant, Arben shot up, his face flushed with rage. He shoved the boy and shouted, "Stop!"

The laughter came to an abrupt halt. The entire class, including

Mr. Modawell, turned their attention to Arben in stunned silence.

"Is there a problem, Mr. Davis?" Mr. Modawell finally asked, his tone calm yet piercing.

Arben stared at the teacher's annoyed expression. He glanced around at everyone staring at him. His fists clenched as he caught sight of the boy he had shoved, now smirking with a sly triumphant grin. A mix of anger and hurt swirled within him, and he could feel himself teetering on the edge of a meltdown. Tilting his head back, he fought to keep the tears from spilling over, his body locked rigidly, fists balled tightly at his sides.

"Sit down, Mr. Davis," the teacher ordered.

But Arben remained rooted in place, his jaw clenched and his frame trembling with suppressed rage. Seeing the fury etched across his face, Mr. Modawell's demeanor softened. "Come with me," he said, gently.

He guided Arben outside the classroom, closing the door behind them. In the quiet hallway, Mr. Modawell turned to him, his voice steady and calm. "Take a deep breath."

Arben exhaled shakily, his breathing uneven as he tried to steady himself. After a few moments, the teacher escorted him to the administration office and left him with the guidance counselor, Mr. Hector.

Mr. Hector sat in silence at first, allowing Arben the space he needed. Eventually, Arben's emotions spilled over. "They throw my stuff on the floor," he sobbed, tears streaming down his face. "They call me names and kick my desk."

Mr. Hector's expression softened as he listened. "I'm sorry, Arben," he said, his tone full of empathy. "No one should treat you like that."

Arben slumped his shoulders, his voice matter-of-factly rather than like a victim. "Mom says I have a devil in me. That's why I hear things, and no one likes me except Ms. Railey."

"I like you," Mr. Hector replied with warmth. "And I'm sure there are others like Ms. Railey and me. I bet your mom was just having a bad day. That happens to all of us sometimes."

Arben knew better. His mother's harsh words haunted him far beyond a single *bad day*. The weight of his home life pressed down on him, and her cutting remarks—*you got the devil in you. God punishes children who disrespect they parents*—echoed relentlessly in his mind.

Mr. Hector continued, "Just like those boys who shouldn't treat you like that. Maybe they were also having a bad day."

"I hate them," Arben burst out. "I didn't do anything to them."

"I know," Mr. Hector assured him. "I'll talk to Mr. Modawell and make sure he keeps an eye on everyone."

Mr. Hector kept Arben in the office for the remainder of the school day, eventually sending him home with a note for his parents that explained the bullying and how it had been addressed.

At home, Arlene read the note and immediately turned on Arben. "Did you provoke them boys? Lord knows you get on my nerves. The Bible says resist the devil, and he will flee from you. Did you act like the devil?"

Arben shook his head but said nothing.

"Listen," Arlene went on, her tone sharp, "You get what you give. If you done somethin' like callin' 'em a name or bein' ugly, then that's what they gonna do back to you. It's called karma. Don't ever do nothin' to no one that you don't want done to you. Understand?"

Feeling her words unfairly placing blame on him, Arben finally said, "I didn't do anything."

"Like that," Arlene snapped. "Right there. You get all mad and backtalk me. You *know* it ain't right to backtalk me. And God says the anger of man does not produce the righteousness of God."

Arben sighed heavily, her words compounding the sense of defeat he already felt. Deciding to avoid further pain, he resolved to keep to himself at school and withdrew further into his own world at home.

Ten

Tarrant County Mental Health Services Center

Tuesday 1:30 pm

After leaving Arben's room for lunch, Dr. Cruz proceeded to the break room next to the doctor's offices.

Drs. Cruz, Hoffman, and Andrews, who often worked with the same patients, frequently used the break room for informal discussions.

Dr. William Hoffman, the most senior member of the team, entered the room last. With more experience than Cruz and Andrews combined, his presence commanded respect. Unlike most staff physicians, he rarely wore the customary white lab coat. Instead, his choice of attire reflected a subdued confidence: outdated brown slacks, a thick-collared shirt, and a cardigan sweater. His thinning gray hair and composed demeanor gave him the distinguished appearance of someone approaching retirement, wise and seasoned.

Heading straight for the vending machine, Dr. Hoffman made a selection and casually tapped his credit card on the payment screen. As he checked his watch, he said, "Look, I've got a packed schedule this week, so I don't see the point in spending much time on the new admit, Arben Davis."

Tearing open a bag of chips, he continued speaking between bites. "I've reviewed the file: hears voices, no friends, paranoid. I'd say there's little doubt he's a schizotypal individual."

"I'm inclined to agree," Dr. Cruz replied. "I need a little more time with him, but it's likely he'll be with us for quite a while."

"I think you're both jumping to conclusions—just like Dr. Campos," Dr. Andrews stated sharply. "Let's do our job and properly evaluate him before rushing to a diagnosis."

Dr. Cruz smirked, a hint of defiance in her expression. "I've already conducted an initial interview, and I stand by what I've said. I agree with Dr. Hoffman. Instead of wasting time asking questions we already know the answers to, we should focus our efforts on creating a cognitive treatment program paired with antipsychotics."

Dr. Hoffman shook his head and said, "Cognitive programs are notoriously difficult to implement on schizophrenics. If you can't silence the voices in his head, you'll always be competing with them."

Dr. Andrews exhaled in frustration. "It's far too early to make *any* definitive recommendation. He has a complex history, and that history will provide far more insight into his behavior than the surface-level interview ever could."

"Stan," Dr. Hoffman began, "we all heard him screaming this

morning in your office. I've also gone through the incident report."

"There's no denying Mr. Davis experienced some kind of episode," Dr. Andrews acknowledged. "But consider the context: not only did he recently lose his mother, he also discovered her decaying body in the backyard. We all know that trauma of that magnitude can manifest in many ways, and it doesn't necessarily point to cognitive impairment. Also, let's not forget he's an accomplished artist. That alone makes it harder to separate his eccentricities from any potential cognitive issues. As I've already said, I believe it's prudent to hold off on a final diagnosis until we've developed a comprehensive profile."

"Stan," Dr. Hoffman said with a mocking snicker, his tone laced with contempt. "I knew you were going to suggest that this young man is simply another eccentric genius." He paused deliberately, letting his words linger. "But seriously, doctor," he continued, "he's hearing voices and tried to kill himself. He even had to be sedated for just walking down the hall."

Dr. Cruz chimed in, "He had another episode when Tyrell tried to lead him into the hallway outside his room." She quickly recounted the incident, detailing how Arben panicked and refused to leave his room because of the loud noise.

"There you have it," Dr. Hoffman said, turning to Dr. Andrews with a triumphant look. "Two documented departures from reality in a single day. As Dr. Cruz suggested, let's begin developing a treatment plan rather than wasting time on further diagnostics."

Dr. Andrews couldn't refute Dr. Hoffman's point but replied firmly, "Will, if that's what he needs then I'll be the first to support it. But please allow me to do the job I was hired to do."

Dr. Hoffman raised an eyebrow, a hint of condescension in his tone. "And when, exactly, will you be doing that?"

"I should be able to see him late Wednesday after rounds or Thursday morning—late Thursday at the latest."

Dr. Hoffman's skepticism was evident as he crossed his arms. "He's only here until Friday morning unless we determine he's a danger, which, frankly, I'm strongly leaning toward."

"You haven't even met him," Dr. Andrews shot back.

"When you've been doing this job as long as I have, you don't always need to meet with the patient," Dr. Hoffman retorted. "I'll be submitting my report by Thursday afternoon. I'm heading out of town and plan to be gone by Friday morning."

Dr. Andrews released a heavy sigh, his frustration palpable. "Just let me complete the background work and meet with him before you submit anything to Campos."

Reluctantly, Dr. Hoffman gave a curt nod. "Fine. As long as you've got everything done by Thursday—preferably in the morning."

"And I suppose there's little chance you'll actually consider the findings in my background report when making your recommendation?" Dr. Andrews asked, narrowing his eyes.

Dr. Hoffman shrugged dismissively. "I'll look at it, but my recommendation will be based on the most immediate clinical observations. As you know, our priority is ensuring the safety of the patient and those around him. Unless you uncover something truly extraordinary… It's unlikely to change my conclusion."

"I may not find a smoking gun, Will, but the totality of this kid's background may be of critical importance."

"Perhaps," Dr. Hoffman said with an indifferent wave. "Get me a summary by Thursday morning, and I'll consider it."

Dr. Andrews nodded, his expression neutral, though internally he wrestled with his disdain for his pompous colleague. Despite the frustration, he resolved to focus on the task at hand—gathering the details that might make a difference for Arben.

Eleven

On the road

2 weeks earlier

In the weeks leading up to Arben's 3-day stay at the Tarrant County Mental Health Services Center, his schedule had become overwhelming. Performance requests flooded in weekly, with eager clients pleading for a slot in his packed calendar. What had initially been a modest two shows per month had rapidly transformed into a demanding workload of four performance per week, sometimes more. The mounting pressure mirrored his rapid ascent but foreshadowed the toll it was taking on him.

Arben's rise to prominence began eleven months earlier, shortly after graduating high school. His professional debut at a Dallas charity benefit captivated the city's elite, who were quick to recognize his extraordinary talent. From that day, he was in demand for corporate events, charitable fund raisers, and upscale parties.

Over the following eleven months, Arben toured nationwide

as a full-time solo pianist. Accompanied by Tova—his agent, manager, and close friend—they drove to local engagements around Dallas/Ft. Worth, where Arben lived with Tova and her husband, and traveled by air to more lucrative performances out of state.

After nearly a year of non-stop playing, traveling, and practicing, the relentless pace was wearing Arben down. While both he and Tova were having the time of their lives, the physical and mental demands of life on the road were exhausting. Arben's growing irritability became harder to ignore, and Tova attributed it to the combined strain of constant travel, lack of sleep, and his persistent hearing issues, which only heightened his frustration.

During their journey to an event in Kansas City, the situation escalated dramatically at the Atlanta airport. Arben, unable to suppress his worsening struggles, reached a breaking point. As they waited for their flight to board, he was once again tormented by a deep agonizing hum. "Stop!" he shouted, his voice echoing through the terminal and turning heads among the crowd of travelers.

Tova, startled by his sudden outburst and the fury in his voice, cautiously asked, "What's wrong?"

Clutching his ears in frustration, Arben shot her a sharp look that screamed, "What do you think?" Without hesitation, Tova rummaged through her bag and produced a pair of earplugs.

"No!" Arben barked, pushing the earplugs away. "I hate this!" he growled, rising abruptly. With trembling hands, he dug into his pocket, pulled out a pair of cotton balls, and shoved them into his ears.

Tova had never witnessed Arben unleash his frustration so

openly. In the past, he had shown mild irritation when sudden loud noises caught him off guard, but he always managed to control his anger and maintain his composure. Now, his emotions were unrestrained. He stormed back and forth, his scowl deepening with every step.

"You're just tired," Tova said softly, her voice calm in an effort to soothe him.

"No. Tired, yes. Tired of loud noises," he snapped.

Uncertain of what else to do, Tova decided to take Arben for a walk around the terminal, hoping to put some distance between them and the aggravating sound. They strolled quietly until they were several gates away from their departing gate.

When they stopped, Tova motioned for Arben to remove the cotton from his ears. "What about now?" she asked. "Is it better?"

"Better, but not gone. I hate this!"

There was no doubt Arben was troubled by the noise, but Tova also noticed the fatigue etched across his face.

"Listen," Tova said gently, choosing her words with care. "We've only got a few more dates before we head home. I think you should take a few days off. Get some rest. Just relax. Okay?"

Arben wasn't ready to let go of his frustration, but as he looked at Tova, he knew he didn't want to direct his anger at her the way his mother used to direct her anger at him.

"Okay," he muttered, but extended his arms to create some distance between them, signaling that he wanted to be left alone.

Finding a quiet spot by the window, Arben stared outside, his mind spiraling. *What is wrong with me?* The question had haunted him for years, elusive and unanswered.

Fatigue and frustration weighed heavily on him, clouding his thoughts. As he watched the planes come and go, his mind wandered before settling on a voice from his past—his mother's sharp, relentless tone, scolding and berating: *Out of the heart comes evil thoughts*, and *God punishes evil.*

His muddled thoughts led him to consider the possibility that his struggles were divine retribution—punishment for some unnamable fault. Alone with his thoughts, his mood darkened further. He felt trapped. *Tova won't like me if I mess up. Without Tova I can't get gigs. Without gigs I have nothing.* The fear of failure loomed large, pushing him to the edge of his own sanity.

God, please, no, he prayed silently, desperate for solace.

Overwhelmed by the crushing tide of thoughts, Arben sank to the terminal floor and buried his head in his hands. Sitting down, however, turned out to be a blessing in disguise. As his eyes closed, exhaustion overcame him, and he drifted into a restless but needed sleep.

From a distance, Tova watched him carefully. When it was finally time to board the flight, she gently roused him and helped him onto the plane where he promptly fell back to sleep. Though Tova longed to do the same, persistent worries about Arben's struggles denied her any peace.

Twelve

Tarrant County Mental Health Services Center

Tuesday 2:00 pm

Dr. Andrews hurried out of the break room, his mind racing after the frustrating exchange with Drs. Hoffman and Cruz. He knew uncovering the events of that day before Arben's suicide attempt was crucial. It was the key to distinguishing between a fleeting bad day and a deeper mental health issue. While the answer would be the end of the diagnostic process, Dr. Andrews knew that it could also provide a starting point for the correct treatment.

Closing his office door, Dr. Andrews immediately dialed Marianne Railey, Arben's piano teacher. Wasting no time, he introduced himself briskly, aware that she had only a brief window between lessons, and he himself was due in the adult psych ward shortly.

"Thank you for making time for this call," Dr. Andrews said.

"My pleasure. I wish I had more time today."

"That's alright. Next time I'll call earlier in the day. I'm hoping to build a complete profile for Arben, but given our limited time, I'd like to focus on recent events."

Intrigued, Marianne replied, "Of course."

"Now, I understand you weren't present at the event when Arben went into the lake."

"That's correct. I was invited but unfortunately, I've been battling the flu."

"I'm sorry to hear that. I hope you're feeling better."

"I am. Thank you."

"So, you spoke with Arben a few days before the event?"

"Yes. He called me the week before, excited."

"Excited about the performance or about seeing you?"

"Both."

"No signs of distress, anger, or anything that suggested he was struggling or in crisis?"

"Nothing. In fact, he sounded better than he had in quite some time."

"Had he been depressed?"

"I wouldn't say depressed, just tired. He and Tova had been working very hard—traveling and playing—and whenever we spoke, he sounded worn out."

"Did you talk to him that day, before or after his mother passed?"

Marianne let out a heavy sigh. "Not that day, but Tova called me that afternoon. She was in a panic."

"This is after he found his mother?"

"Yes. Tova had been there at his mother's house and said

Arben was very upset."

"Understandably."

"Of course, but later, when she called me, Arben was getting dressed for the performance. She said he was calm, as if nothing had happened. Tova didn't know what to do."

"Didn't know what to do about what?" Dr. Andrews asked.

"She was confused. Just hours earlier, he'd been utterly distraught, and now he was calmly preparing for a performance. She wasn't sure if he should see a doctor, cancel the performance, or if he might have another breakdown right in the middle of it." She paused, her voice unsteady as tears welled up. "And, I guess she was right to worry."

"I understand. But before that day, had you ever seen Arben so distraught or unstable that it made you concerned?"

"Hmph," she grunted. "I was always worried about Arben."

"Why is that?" Dr. Andrews asked, leaning back in his chair, prepared to listen as Marianne began reflecting on her observations of Arben over the last decade.

Thirteen

On the road

2 weeks earlier

Unable to find rest on the plane, unlike Arben, Tova's mind remained troubled by the incident earlier in the airport terminal. As the plane ascended and Arben again sleeping, her thoughts turned to the past few weeks on the road. The long hours and erratic schedule—late-night performances, early morning departures, eating at odd hours, and nights spent in unfamiliar beds—had drained them both physically and mentally. Adding to the strain, the increasingly enthusiastic and consequently louder crowds were only worsening Arben's struggle with hearing pain.

Tova had been picking up on the subtle yet troubling signs of Arben's deterioration: his moods darkening, twisting and turning more frequently.

As the plane prepared for final descent, Tova gently woke him. By the time they arrived at their hotel in Kansas City, Arben seemed to have bounced back from his earlier meltdown. Yet, deep down, Tova couldn't shake the sinking feeling that his improvement was temporary.

Before Arben's final performance in Kansas City, Tova hesitantly suggested he try wearing earplugs. Tears welled up in his eyes, and with heart-wrenching sorrow, he said, "I don't want to play if I have to wear them."

The anguish in his voice and the despair in his expression struck Tova deeply, intensifying her worry. She couldn't, in good conscience, stand by and allow Arben to jeopardize his hearing. Yet, she knew how much performing live meant to him—it was everything.

Occasionally, Tova had seen Arben put cotton balls in his ears before a performance in an attempt to manage the pain, but the muffled sound seemed to frustrate him more than the discomfort. By the second song, he would inevitably remove them, choosing to endure the pain rather than compromise the clarity of the music.

After Kansas City, Arben pushed through two more performances in different cities before they finally returned to Ft. Worth for some much-needed rest. They arrived at Tova's house late at night, where Arben dropped his luggage just inside the front door and made a beeline for the bed.

Over the next several days, he slept deeply each night, falling asleep early—usually before ten—and spent most of his waking hours lounging and napping often. For the first time in weeks, the exhaustion visibly eased on his face, offering Tova a glimmer of relief.

Within days, Arben resumed his normal routine—rising

early to practice the piano. Rested and cheerful, he appeared far more relaxed. Yet, as his energy returned, so did his restlessness. Before long, he began begging Tova to get them back on the road.

After nearly a week off, Tova delivered the news Arben had been hoping for—along with a special surprise. "I confirmed some new dates for next week," she announced.

Arben's face lit up instantly.

"Guess where we're going?" she teased with a mischievous smile and raised eyebrows.

Arben gave her a suspicious look but didn't say a word.

"Austin."

Arben's hometown.

His eyes widened with delight. "Really?"

"First, we've got an event in Florida," she continued, "but the following weekend you're booked at a private party on Lake Travis. Do you know where that is?"

He nodded eagerly, his excitement overflowing. "I can go home."

"Maybe you can invite your mother."

Arben's giddiness grew. "Yes! She can hear me play."

"And what about your piano teacher, Ms. Railey?"

"Yes. Yes!" he exclaimed, practically bursting with joy. He quickly pulled out his cellphone. "I'm going to call them."

While Arlene didn't answer, Ms. Railey was thrilled to hear that Arben was coming home. "I can't wait to see you," she said warmly. "Please text me the address and I'll be there."

In the days that followed, Arben was practically walking on air. Though his mother had never seen him perform, he was certain she wanted to. Even though she hadn't responded to his calls or texts, Arben held onto the hope that she would show up. Their estrangement since his move a year ago following a heated and violent argument weighed on him. But with his career now thriving, Arben saw this as the perfect opportunity to reconnect and mend the rift.

Fourteen

Tarrant County Mental Health Services Center

Tuesday 2:00 pm

After Marianne Railey briefly recounted her conversation with Tova just hours before Arben's suicide attempt, Dr. Andrews listened attentively, waiting as she began to reflect on the concerns she had carried for him and the reasons behind them.

"I've worried about Arben almost from the day we met—over ten years ago," Marianne said, her tone soft as she paused to recall her earliest memory of him. "From the moment he first sat beside me at the piano, it was clear he was extraordinary. I've never met a more gifted musician."

Dr. Andrews, intrigued, asked, "When did you first begin to worry about him, and what caused your concern?"

"Almost immediately," she admitted with a reflective sigh. "Sweet little Arben stepped out of the car for his first lesson. I was teaching out of my grandmother's house in Austin at the time, and he must have been about six or seven. His family lived about five miles away, so his mother drove him to that first lesson. After that, though, she rarely brought him."

"How did Arben get back and forth?"

"City bus. It broke my heart seeing how those people mistreated that little angel. Can you imagine? A six, seven, eight-year-old boy navigating through such a dangerous process on his own. I prayed for him every day. He was always so eager to play, but that mother of his…" She hesitated before adding, "I shouldn't speak ill of the dead, but she really made Arben grow up too fast."

"How so?"

She paused, choosing her words carefully. "Listen, I know you're trying to help Arben but as a Christian, I don't feel right airing someone else's dirty laundry."

"I understand, but remember, this isn't about gossip or judgement. It's about understanding."

"No, I know. Okay, so, Arben's first lesson. I was outside when his mother dropped him off at the end of the driveway. I introduced myself and invited her in, but she declined and sped away. She never once set foot in my house. When she *did* pick him up, she was always hours late. I didn't mind, though. I was glad he had a safe place to stay, even if his parents were using me as a babysitter."

"A safe place. Was his place unsafe?"

"He lived in a pretty rough part of town but honestly, the real danger was inside the house."

"His parents?"

"Yes, but it was more than that. For example, at Arben's

first recital—when he was about thirteen—his aunt showed up so drunk she could barely stand."

"Which had to be embarrassing for Arben."

"I'm sure it was," Marianne said. "But he took it in stride. Still, after the recital, his aunt was nowhere to be found, and she was supposed to drive him home."

"And I'm guessing you gave him a ride?"

"I offered but he declined. I think he was too proud—or maybe ashamed—to accept. But I couldn't just leave him there, alone on the dark parking lot of Austin High School, so I stayed with him. Lo and behold a car finally pulled up." She paused, taking a steadying breath. "And there she was, Arben's aunt, hanging halfway out of the passenger-side window slurring her words. 'Hey Arbs,' she called out. 'C'mon.' I could barely understand her."

"Passenger side, so she wasn't driving?"

"No. The car stopped and out stepped this rough-looking man. 'Get in,' he barked, glaring at Arben. I have to admit, I was tempted to intervene, but honestly… the man scared me."

"Did Arben get in?"

"He stared at the man for a moment—it was awful. I could see that Arben was scared. Then the man shouted, 'Get in, dumb…'" She hesitated, her voice trembling. "I don't want to repeat the word he used, but it wasn't kind. I wanted so badly to help Arben but I couldn't. I was too afraid, and I didn't want to get in the middle of a family dispute." She sighed heavily. "It broke my heart to watch Arben climb into that car, but what choice did I have?"

"None," Dr. Andrews said softly.

"As they sped off, I caught a glimpse of his aunt, her head

flopping against the window. I'm pretty sure she was passed out."

"Wow."

"There's no telling what happened after that," Marianne continued, her voice filled with regret. "So, you see, it wasn't just Arben's parents. It was everything—the environment, their friends, the drugs, the neighborhood—all of it."

"I can certainly see why that would have been difficult to witness."

"Like I said, I always worried about Arben. I even think his mother was drunk when she dropped him off that first day." She paused and let out a disdainful snort as she recalled the moments of disgust she'd felt for Arlene over the years. "Her eyes were red, her words slurred, and the smell of alcohol was overwhelming. And that wasn't the only time. More than once, Arben missed his lesson because, as he put it, 'Mom is sick.'"

"And sick meant?"

"Drunk, hungover, passed out—who knows exactly. But Arben made it clear that she wasn't in a condition to take care of herself."

Fifteen

Arben's childhood home, Austin, Texas

5 years earlier

Not long after his father's passing, 15-year-old Arben came home from school to find the house eerily quiet. He checked the kitchen and den but found no one. He wondered if his mother and aunt had caught a ride somewhere, perhaps a bar, leaving him home alone. For a brief moment, he felt a surge of excitement, thinking he could practice the piano as much as he wanted without being told to stop.

"Mom?" he called out. He stuck his head into her bedroom and found her sprawled on the bed, lying in her own vomit. He'd seen her passed out drunk countless times and, disgusted, turned to leave, expecting she'd sleep it off. However, just as he was about to close the door, he heard a deep, guttural cough—not her normal smoker's hack, but something far worse.

He stood in the doorway, and she coughed again, but it

sounded more like a gurgle. Foam bubbled from her mouth—she was choking on her own vomit. "Mom!" he shouted, panic rising. Suddenly, her body heaved violently, then went still.

Arben rushed to her side, pulling her upright. "Mom!" he shouted again. She was limp like a rag doll, her chest heaving with no air coming through. Desperately, he remembered the Heimlich maneuver from school. Positioning himself behind her, he gave her a sharp, forceful squeeze. Fluid sprayed from her mouth, splattering across the room. She began to cough, her breathing ragged but steady. Arlene was too intoxicated to stay upright, so she fell back onto the bed and closed her eyes, but she was breathing.

Arben raced to the bathroom, soaked a rag in cold water, and rubbed it across her face. She started to come around but again fell back and closed her eyes. "No! Mom!" he yelled, shaking her. She barely raised her lids and looked at him through swirling eyes, seeming to recognize him, letting out a faint grunt.

Arben grabbed the phone. "I'm calling 911."

Arlene slapped the cellphone out of his hand with what little coherence she had mustered. "No," she slurred.

"Mom, I'm calling," he insisted, releasing her to retrieve his phone.

"No!" she cried. "I'm… I'm…" Her words trailed off as she rolled over and attempted to push herself up. "Don't call."

Arben steadied her, but her legs buckled beneath her. "Mom, you need help."

"They'll lock me up… take you away."

"No, they won't," he replied, unsure if it was true, but not caring if it was. However, Arben set his phone down without calling 911.

He sat her on the bed and re-soaked the rag in cold water, pressing it to her face. The cold water jolted her slightly, bringing her closer to consciousness.

For the next few hours, Arben stayed by her side, keeping his mother upright as she slowly came back to life. She vomited repeatedly, and each time, he cleaned up without hesitation. By midnight, Arlene was hunched over a trashcan, her body wracked with exhaustion. "I'm sorry, Arby," she whispered. She looked ten years older—her hair clung to her face in sweat-soaked strands, her makeup smeared across her face and the sheets, and her bloodshot eyes were sunken like those of someone terminally ill. Her head pounded, and her vision was cloudy at best.

"I don't know what happened," she murmured. Her words were sluggish and fragmented. "I was listenin' to a tape of Benny's last performance." She stared into the putrid trashcan, her expression distant, before slowly shaking her head. "I just can't let go, Arby. I'm sorry."

Arben wrapped an arm around her, holding her as she wept. Eventually, exhaustion overtook her and she fell asleep leaning against him. He sat beside the bed for the rest of the night, watching over her to make sure she was okay.

That wasn't the last time Arlene drank herself into a dangerous state, and it wasn't the last time Arben was there to pick up the pieces.

Sixteen

Tarrant County Mental Health Services Center

Tuesday 2:30 pm

Dr. Andrews found his conversation with Ms. Railey very helpful in shedding light on Arben's troubled upbringing.

"Did you ever witness any *physical* abuse?" he asked.

"I never saw her hit him," Ms. Railey replied. "But there were signs."

When she didn't continue, Dr Andrews gently pressed, "Signs?"

"Arben never played sports or did anything physical, but he'd often show up with bruises on his arms, red marks on his face, and I noticed several times he'd wince when he sat on the piano bench. I think they beat that sweet little boy on a regular basis."

"Mmm," Dr. Andrews murmured, pained by what he was hearing. "Did you ever consider contacting Child Protective Services?"

Ms. Railey took a few deep breaths as emotion swelled within her. "Lord knows, I wanted to. I prayed every night for the strength to save that little boy, to do the right thing—whatever that was. And I prayed for God to give Arben the strength to make it through."

She choked up, remorse and regret tightening their grip. "But I didn't. I just couldn't bring myself to step between a mother and her son. It broke my heart."

"You never reported it?"

"I couldn't."

"Why not?"

She went silent, struggling to find the words.

"Marianne?"

"Oh God, why didn't I?" she cried, her voice breaking as she dissolved into tears.

"Do you want to take a moment? We can continue later if you'd prefer."

Ms. Railey sniffled and pulled herself together. "No. I'm fine. I couldn't report it because she would've taken it out on Arben, and I was afraid I'd never see him again."

"What made you think that?"

"Arben used to repeat the things his mother said to him: 'You've got a devil inside you,' 'God punishes evil thoughts,' and 'Disobedient children get eaten by vultures.'"

"What?"

"I know," Ms. Railey murmured. "She had a way of twisting and distorting scripture, using it as a weapon to punish him. At least that's what I think. Arben grew up hearing a lot of awful messages about how God disapproved of him and wanted to punish him."

She paused, taking a deep breath. "As a Christian, I couldn't stand by and let him believe that God hated him. I started teaching him from the Bible myself, trying to undo the *distortions* she'd planted in his mind. I wanted him to know that God didn't hate him—He loves him."

"That's sounds like a good thing."

"It was—until Arlene found out."

"She didn't approve?"

Marianne let out a bitter snort, her frustration fueling a renewed strength. "One day Arlene confronted me. 'I don't want you fillin' my son's head full a B.S.,' she said. I took it in stride and calmly replied, 'I understand.' I thought that was that, but then she launched into a tirade that scared me. I honestly thought she was going to attack me physically. 'I ain't foolin' around,' she said, poking me in the chest with her finger. 'You better stop fillin' his head with religion or I swear to God I'll…' She paused before finishing that threat, but I'll never forget what she said next. 'I'll cancel his lessons in a heartbeat, and you'll never see Arben again.'"

The memory sent Ms. Railey back into tears. "I've never been so scared in my life. Arlene had always been aloof, and occasionally nice, but this… this was like nothing I'd ever seen."

"And if you would've called the police or CPS?"

"Those people are so overburdened. What would they have done? The police *might* have written a report. CPS *could've* investigated, but it wouldn't have changed much. She—his mother—would've known it was me who filed the complaint. And poor little Arben… he'd still be left alone with her, day after day, facing what I faced that one time. I just couldn't do that to him."

Her crying deepened into a wail, the pain she'd carried for so long pouring out all at once. After a few minutes, she fought to regain her composure. "I'm sorry doctor. Can we finish this later?"

"Yes, of course. Again, I am truly sorry for what you've been through. And if you need someone to talk to, I'm here—anytime."

"Thank you," she whispered before hanging up.

Dr. Andrews sat for a long moment, replaying their conversation in his mind. He scribbled a few notes, attempting to piece together the fragmented narrative of Arben's life—the challenges he had faced, the confusing and harmful beliefs instilled in him during his formative years. As he reflected, Dr. Andrews considered how these trials had shaped Arben, molding him into the young man who now found himself confined within the walls of a mental institution, struggling to understand a world that had brought him so much sorrow.

Seventeen

Tarrant County Mental Health Services Center

Tuesday 2:45 pm

Arben was gazing through the window at the courtyard outside his room at the TCMHSC. He turned sharply and reached for his ears when the door opened and in walked a friendly-looking young woman wearing scrubs, accompanied by Tyrell.

"Hello Arben," the young woman said as she and Tyrell quickly stepped inside and shut the door. "My name is Katrine."

She held up a small serving tray containing two cups. "I brought you some medication that will help you relax."

Arben gave her a suspicious look, remembering how they had drugged him earlier. "I don't need that," he said, his tone firm.

Katrine smiled. "Oh, this is a very mild dose. It'll help you feel better."

He considered saying no, but her gentle demeanor and reassuring smile softened his resolve, and he reluctantly gave in.

She approached Arben, still standing at the window, and handed him a tiny paper cup that contained a single dose of an anti-anxiety medication. He popped the pill in his mouth and followed it with the cup of water she handed him.

"Very good, Arben. Thank you." She took the empty cups and added, "Dr. Cruz will be in shortly. Is there anything I can bring you? A soda, perhaps, or maybe a snack?"

Arben shook his head.

After Katrine and Tyrell left, Arben's attention drifted back to the courtyard just beyond the window. The desolate scene deepened his sense of isolation. He wanted to leave but had nowhere to go.

His once-thriving musical career was in limbo. His parents were both gone. And Tova, one of his only friends, was likely mad at him for the incident in Austin.

He sighed, the weight of loneliness and aimlessness pressing heavily on his spirit.

Before long, the medication began to take effect, sending a tingling wave through his body and causing his thoughts to wander.

He was startled as Dr. Cruz made a sudden entrance. She quickly shut the door and said, "Hello again, Arben. Are you ready to talk a little more?"

He shrugged and moved slowly toward the bed where he perched on its edge.

Dr. Cruz studied him closely, looking for signs that he was fully medicated: a relaxed posture, slowed blinking, and deep, unhurried breathing. Satisfied that he was calm enough to delve into sensitive topics, she settled into the lone chair beside the bed.

Dr. Cruz had read in Arben's file that he had been hearing

voices since childhood, a rarity that piqued her professional curiosity. This detail held potential clues to understanding his current state of mind.

"Great. Earlier, we talked about your childhood in Austin and how you learned to play the piano." She paused to swipe her tablet to a note-taking screen. "You mentioned having a friend named Olivia. Tell me about her—how did you two meet?"

Arben delved into his memory, recalling the day he and Olivia became friends.

Eighteen

Overton Elementary School, Austin, Texas

12 years earlier

Eight-year-old Arben was sitting alone, as he always did, on the playground of Overton Elementary School. Olivia, a classmate with thick glasses and an awkward gait caused by her underdeveloped legs, hobbled toward him. Because of her disability, Olivia always tried to stay unnoticed, sticking to the perimeters and staying in the shadows to avoid drawing attention.

Initially, Arben ignored Olivia, as he did with anyone unfamiliar. However, it only took a moment for him to recognize that Olivia posed no threat.

He glanced up and said, "I'm Arben."

She lowered her head, pushed her glasses up, and shyly flashed a half-wave. "Olivia. Do you always play here?" she asked softly.

"I play music and talk to stuff," Arben replied casually.

"Uh-huh. What do you mean?"

Arben stood and cupped his hand behind his ear. "Hear that bird?"

She listened for a moment, then nodded. "Uh-huh."

"Some birds sing and some talk."

The bird chirped three distinctive notes. Arben listened carefully, remarking after each chirp, "A-flat. A. A-flat."

"What's a flat?"

"Not a flat," Arben said, smiling. "A-flat."

"I don't get it. Can you—" She suddenly stopped when a group of bullies approached: four boys and one girl.

"Hey, look," Virgil, the leader of the bullies, said. "It's the spaz and the re-tard, together. Maybe they'll make spaz-tard babies."

Olivia slunk behind Arben as the group erupted in cruel laughter.

Despite his nervousness, Arben remained stone-faced. He could feel Olivia's trembling hand clutching his shirt, her fear palpable as she shrank behind him. Having been bullied many times himself, Arben felt a deep kinship with Olivia.

Drawing in a steadying breath, Arben stood tall, his fear giving way to quiet but fierce courage. "Stop!" he demanded, his voice firm and unwavering.

Virgil stepped close to Arben and poked him in the chest. "I don't take orders from re-tards." With a sudden shove, he sent Arben stumbling backwards into Olivia, knocking her to the ground. The group laughed as Virgil taunted, "Watch her get up."

Olivia rolled onto her stomach, her movements clumsy and strained as she struggled to get up. The bullies' laughter grew louder.

Watching Olivia's humiliation unfold, Arben felt a sharp pang of empathy. Her helplessness mirrored his own past experiences. A surge of outrage built within him as he clenched his fists, his resolve hardening.

Olivia finally managed to get to her feet and hobbled toward the school as quickly as she could. "Run Forrest," Virgil shouted after her, his taunt drawing delighted laughter from his crew.

Arben turned to face the bullies, his emotions boiling over. "Stop!" he screamed, his voice raw and thunderous. The sheer intensity of his outburst startled everyone, including himself. The laughter ceased abruptly, replaced with stunned silence.

Overwhelmed by the moment, Arben started welling up. He quickly turned his back to the bullies so they couldn't see his vulnerability. Lowering his head, he pushed past the group and hurried to catch up with Olivia. Just before reaching her, he wiped his eyes, erasing the evidence of his emotions.

"You didn't have to do that," she whispered.

Arben shrugged and walked her inside without another word.

Nineteen

Tarrant County Mental Health Services Center

Tuesday 3:30 pm

Arben snapped back to the present as Dr. Cruz's face came into focus. She had been waiting for him to respond to her question, but his blank stare revealed that the medication was affecting his ability to pay attention.

"Olivia was your best friend growing up," Dr. Cruz reiterated. "What kind of things did you and Olivia talk about?"

The memory of Olivia was very special to Arben, something he wasn't ready to share with Dr. Cruz.

He shrugged. "We talked about stuff."

"Did you talk to her about the voices you heard?"

Arben silently studied the doctor, his expression unreadable. Beneath the surface, irritation crept in. *You won't understand and you can't fix it*, he thought.

"Arben?" Dr. Cruz prompted as his silence stretched on, only offering a long, vacant stare.

"Olivia left," he muttered, hoping to close the subject.

"You said you didn't have a lot of friends, so it must have been hard to see her go."

Arben nodded absently, his eyes wandering around the room. The powerful medication coursing through his system made it difficult to focus on a single thought. He blinked a few times unnecessarily.

Instinctively he patted his pocket, feeling the familiar outline of the letter Olivia had penned many years ago. He always kept it close.

Twenty

Overton Elementary School, Austin, Texas

12 years earlier

After their initial run-in with the bullies, Arben and Olivia became inseparable friends. Recess became their sacred time together, spent sitting in the same spot where they had first met, sharing stories and doodling in the dirt.

One afternoon, Arben turned to Olivia and said, "I talk to the wishing trees."

"What are wishing trees?"

"They're in my backyard. They tell me to wish, wish, wish."

Olivia's eyes sparkled, as if Arben had a magical genie. "What do you wish for?"

Feeling comfortable with Olivia, Arben casually replied, "I wish I could play the piano all the time."

"You should wish for something good, like ice cream," Olivia teased with a grin.

Arben paused, considering her words before shaking his head slightly. "That's not how it works."

"Why not? Do you ever get your wish?"

Arben shrugged nonchalantly. "Sometimes they talk and sometimes I talk. They say 'wish,' but I don't think they can make it come true."

"You talk?"

He nodded confidently. "To the swing, the trees, the birds—lots of things." His matter-of-fact tone left no room for doubt, as if such conversations were the most natural thing in the world.

"But you said the birds sing. You said A-flat."

Arben chuckled at her unfamiliarity with music.

"They sometimes *sing* A-flat. Listen," he said, pausing and inviting her to listen to the nearby birds.

After one chirped a familiar pattern, Arben repeated what he heard. "Did it. Did it. Did it."

He looked at her with a knowing smile. "See?"

"How do you know when they're talking and when they're singing?"

Arben thought for a moment. Finally, he casually said, "I just hear it."

Tilting his head slightly, he focused on a distant sound. "Hear that?"

"The birds?" Olivia guessed, leaning closer, trying to hear what he was hearing.

He shook his head and pointed toward the horizon. "Over there. You hear a lot of people talking?"

Olivia listened intently but then shook her head. "What are

they saying?"

"I can't tell," Arben admitted. "I hear them in my backyard."

Day after day, they would meet at the same spot, sharing stories, playing together, and sticking close together whenever the bullies came near. For months, they were best friends, sharing thoughts, dreams, and even a few secrets.

But their time together came to an abrupt end when Olivia announced she was leaving. She had missed classes for a few days, and suddenly appeared on the playground during recess. As she approached, Arben knew by the look on her face that something was terribly wrong.

"You missed show-and-tell," he said, his voice faltering as he struggled to respond to her troubled expression.

She stared at him with eyes brimming with sadness. "Mom and me are moving," she said softly

"Where?"

She shrugged, her sadness suddenly shifting to fear. "You can't tell anyone," she said, her voice barely above a whisper.

Arben was baffled, but instinctively knew not to ask why. He nodded solemnly, promising to keep her secret without understanding the full weight of what it might be.

Then, Olivia slid the sleeve of her shirt up, revealing several bruises on her arm. She looked Arben in the eye as he stared at her wounds.

Arben subconsciously ran a hand over his own bruises, understanding what Olivia was telling him. He wanted to stop whoever was hurting her, but he knew it was far beyond his control.

He wiped the single tear before it slid down his face, wishing he could release his feelings and cry for both of them.

The silence was broken when Olivia spoke with a quiver in her voice. "I don't wanna go, but Mom said we have to. Daddy's…" Her words trailed off as she choked on her emotions, slowly shaking her head with her eyes closed.

"You can't go," Arben pleaded, desperate to keep his best friend.

Olivia's shoulders slumped, her gaze dropping to the ground. Then, as if struck by urgency, her head shot up and her wide eyes darted around. "Mom's inside getting my lessons. She told me not to go far. I have to go."

"Now?" Arben asked, jumping up to help her up. His hand gripped her arm, and she winced sharply. "Ouch," she cried, as Arben's fingers pressed another sore spot.

"I'm sorry," he said, quickly releasing his grip.

"I know," she replied softly, straightening herself up while keeping her doleful eyes fixed on him. "I don't wanna go," she repeated, her voice filled with a haunting finality that tore at Arben's heart.

"When are you coming back?"

She woefully shook her head and whispered, "I'm not."

Her words hit Arben like a punch to the stomach, leaving him breathless. He stared at her as tears began to fill the corners of his eyes. He leaned his head back, trying to blink them away, but his emotions surged. He wanted to stay strong, but it was too much.

"I don't want you to go," he managed to say.

Olivia hesitated, then reached into her pocket and pulled out a small, folded piece of paper. Without a word, she handed it to him.

Arben took the paper, but his eyes never left her.

"I wrote you a letter."

In that fleeting moment, Arben couldn't fully process her words. He clutched the paper tightly as though holding onto it could somehow keep her from leaving.

The image of Olivia walking away, her sleeves hiding the bruises she had trusted him to see became an indelible mark in his memory.

Twenty-One

Tarrant County Mental Health Services Center

Tuesday 4:00 pm

Dr. Cruz's voice gently broke through Arben's haze, pulling him back to the present. She had been patiently waiting for him to share more about his memories of Olivia. She hoped that revisiting those moments might provide a path to discussing the voices he had heard as a child.

As Arben stared at the doctor, she observed the sad, distant expression on his face.

Softly, Dr. Cruz said, "Would you like to take a break, or would you prefer to continue talking about Olivia and your childhood?"

Arben gave no response. The vivid memory of Olivia, entwined with the fog brought on by the medication brought a tear to his eye. He wiped it quickly, lowering his head as if to shield his emotions. After a long pause, he slowly nodded, signaling that he was ready to continue.

Still guarded, he rubbed his arm absentmindedly, murmuring, "Her dad was mean."

"Sometimes a strict father can seem like he's being mean," the doctor offered. She watched Arben closely, gauging whether her words would encourage him to share more or retreat further into his silence.

"What about your father?" Dr. Cruz asked. "Was he ever mean?"

At the mention of his father, Arben's thoughts drifted into the past. He stared into space for a moment before suddenly shouting, "Stop!"

Startled, Dr. Cruz tensed, then remained steady, waiting for his next move.

The medication coursing through Arben made it possible for him to hear and understand Dr. Cruz's words, but his thoughts were chaotic, like trying to follow a conversation while being absorbed in an intense, all-consuming show.

"He told you to stop playing?" Dr. Cruz asked.

"Sometimes."

"What happened if you disobeyed him?"

Arben's response came almost like a reflex. The word *disobey* triggered a flood of memories, each tied to the warnings from his mother and their looming consequences. "God will send you to hell," he said softly.

Dr. Cruz had counseled numerous patients experiencing mental challenges and disturbances, many of whom linked their trauma to demons, hell, and divine retribution. Thus, Arben's sentiments were not unexpected.

"Did your father hit you?"

Arben's eyes locked on to the doctor, though his mind was far away, replaying the first time Benny's violence erupted. The memories were vivid and the pain felt as fresh as ever.

Twenty-Two

Arben's childhood home, Austin, Texas

14 years earlier

"Stop!" Benny shouted at six-year-old Arben, who was seated at the piano. He had been practicing Ms. Railey's lessons incessantly.

"Dad, I have to practice."

"No more. You've been bangin' that thing all damn day."

Arben glanced at his father across the room, then back at the piano. He couldn't resist. Playing wasn't just a habit for him, it was his obsession, a sanctuary he couldn't bring himself to leave.

In an instant, Benny jumped to his feet, unbuckled his belt, and whipped it off. The chilling sound of leather slapping violently as the belt slid though the loops would forever haunt Arben. It was a sound that would follow him for years, triggering the same wave of fear every time he heard something similar.

Benny flew across the room in a rage, grabbed Arben off the

piano bench, and struck him repeatedly with the belt. The pain came in sharp, searing waves, but it was the sound of his own screams that left him shaken to his core. He turned to his mother, silently pleading for her intervention, but her expression remained unchanged.

"You shoulda listened to your daddy," Arlene said, her words cold and detached as Benny practically tossed Arben into the backyard.

The betrayal stung as much as the belt. That moment burned into Arben's memory a haunting mix of terror, pain, and the unshakable question: *Why didn't Mom help me?*

Twenty-Three

Tarrant County Mental Health Services Center

Tuesday 4:00 pm

Sitting in silence with Dr. Cruz, Arben wrestled with the terrible memory he could never escape. "The belt," he murmured.

"He hit you with a belt?" Dr. Cruz asked, her voice steady yet concerned.

Her question played like a voiceover, pulling Arben back to the painful memory of being a six-year-old, standing helpless at the mercy of Benny's wrath. He slowly glanced around the room, as if he were looking around the backyard where he'd been exiled while his father's anger raged on inside. Slowly, he emerged from his trance and stared at Dr. Cruz without answering.

Dr. Cruz had seen many patients disappear into their own thoughts when heavily medicated. She patiently watched, periodically checking her phone as Arben zoned out before reengaging, his eyes wide and breathing heavily.

She put her phone away and resumed their session. "Arben, let's talk about the voices you hear."

He looked away. "You won't understand. And you can't fix it."

"Arben, I *want* to understand, and I want to help you. But you have to talk to me."

He gave no response.

She waited through a long silence before trying a different approach. "Do you remember when you first heard voices?"

Arben stared into the distance before murmuring, "Wiissshhh."

Dr. Cruz furrowed her brow. "Wish?" she repeated quizzically. "What does that mean? Were you wishing for something?"

"The trees said wiissshhh," he replied, his voice a whisper.

"Okay," she said, intrigued. "And what else did they say?"

Arben hesitated, wrestling with the chaotic stream of thoughts the medication brought on. Yet, her question lingered in his mind, unlocking a rare moment of clarity. "They kept talking," he said.

"The trees?"

He gave a hesitant nod.

"What did you do when they said 'wish'?"

"I said stop."

"Did they?"

Irritated, he said, "No."

"We're you afraid?"

"Yes," he said sharply. His mind churned, cycling through all the times he'd confessed to hearing the sounds—only to be met with disbelief. He knew the doctor wouldn't believe him either, or would dismiss his story as the product of exceptional hearing or an overactive imagination.

"Do you remember what you did after that?" she pressed.

The day he first heard the voices came rushing back. His eyes widened as the scene replayed in his mind: the confusion that froze him, the fleeting curiosity, and finally, the fear. "I ran inside and hid in the closet."

"What did your parents say when you told them about the voices?"

Arben could still hear his mother's response echoing in his mind when he told her there was someone in the backyard: *There ain't nothin' out there, and God's gonna punish you for makin' up lies.*

He sighed, sinking back into the memories of not being believed or dismissed. He shrugged, hoping the doctor would change the subject.

"And you and your mother had a good relationship before you left home?"

Dr. Cruz's question derailed Arben's fixation on the voices in the backyard. He furrowed his brow trying to form an answer. His mother had always criticized him, blaming his misfortune on his thoughts and actions. She had missed all his performances, hated his taste in music, but never refused his help when she was hungover or in the throes of an overdose. It was never a *good* relationship, as Dr. Cruz put it.

Frustration surged through Arben once again. "She hit me," he snapped. "I left, but she needed me."

His breathing increased, his torturous thoughts bounced between love and resentment, confusion and clarity, and anger and guilt. Dr. Cruz watched him carefully, noting the intensity of his emotions. "You left to follow your career as a musician," Dr. Cruz remarked.

Arben's jaw tightened. "She hit me."

"For leaving home?"

"No. She was with a man—he didn't even know her name. I didn't like it and she hit me."

"And that's when you decided to leave?"

"She hit me and I left. But she needed me." His tone shifted from anger to sorrow. He was mentally exhausted and his emotions were raw and overworked.

Dr. Cruz nodded, understanding the complexity of his emotions. "It's okay to feel conflicted, Arben. You did what you had to do to protect yourself."

He gave no response through a long silence

"Was that the last time you saw her?"

He let out a deep sigh, his tone defeated, "I called and she got mad. She hung up. I called again and again."

Dr. Cruz studied him closely, sensing the depth of his pain and the weight of his unresolved guilt. "When she hit you—was that the last time you saw her?"

His shoulders slumped as he stared blankly at the floor. "In the yard," he murmured.

"You're not responsible for her passing, Arben," Dr. Cruz said softly.

She glanced down at her notes, swiping through. "I think we're about finished," she said, thinking, *Classic SPD* (Schizotypal Personality Disorder) *dissociative, numerous deep-seated conflicts—*

he'll needs long-term care.

"I want you to relax. We're going to help you work all these things out."

"I want to go home."

Dr. Cruz didn't want to tell him that wasn't going to happen for a long time. "I know," she said softly. "Why don't you get some rest?" She stood and made her way to the door.

He stretched out on the bed and mumbled, "I want to go home."

Dr. Cruz darted out the door before he could cover his ears.

Twenty-Four

Residence of Tova and David Rawlins

10 days earlier

After nearly a year of touring and an emotional breakdown at the Atlanta airport, Arben and Tova took a well-deserved seven-day break at Tova's house.

As Arben prepared for the performance in his hometown, the excitement of seeing his mother again grew stronger.

On the morning of their departure, both Arben and Tova felt rested and ready to tackle their busy schedule once more. A few hours before they were set to leave, Tova made a quick run to the store while Arben decided to call his mother. He had reached out numerous times over the past few months, but they hadn't spoken since the day he left home after she struck him for making a crass remark.

Arben was surprised when she answered.

"Mom, it's me."

"Hello Arben." Her voice was cold and distant.

"I've been on the road playing, and I'm making money."

She had often criticized him for winning piano competitions that didn't award substantial prize money. Now that his career was taking off, he hoped she would be impressed or at least respect the fact that he was earning a living.

"It's really fun," he added, nervously pacing around Tova's den.

"That's fine, son," Arlene said in a flat, disinterested tone.

"I have a gig in Austin, so I'm coming home."

"Arben, this ain't your home no more."

"But I live there."

"You *used* to live here."

Arben had never been good at arguing, especially with his domineering mother.

"Okay. I'm coming home next week."

"You ain't gotta come here. I'm doin' fine." She paused then added, "I been busy too, but that really ain't none a your business."

"Oh. Okay," Arben said quietly, his resolve slipping away.

After a long, uneasy silence, Arlene continued, "Arby, you hurt me. Hurt me bad. You run off, just left me, right when I needed you most. I raised you, and you just up and throw'd me away. And what you done? Takin' up with that married woman, disrespectin' me, your own mother, and abandonin' your home—you know that was wrong. Someday you're gonna have to answer to God for what you done."

She paused again, taking a few deep breaths.

"Now you 'spect to just waltz back in here like nothin'

happened? Life don't work like that."

Arben wanted to protest, but she had power over him.

"I'm sor—"

"I ain't hearin' that, Arben," she cut in sharply. "Sorry's all you ever got. I done told you too many times—'bout karma, 'bout not gettin' full a yourself, 'bout what happens when you do bad things, breakin' God's commandments, and ignorin' His will. You know better. If you had manners—any a the morals I taught you—if you cared about me at all, you wouldn't a left."

She began to choke up, struggling with each word. "'Member, it was *you* that left—just like my daddy, just like my sister, and just like Benny. Not me. And… You know what? I'm done." She hung up.

Arben felt the weight of her words hit him like a wave. He paced around the room, trying to process his swirling emotions. Initially, he was furious, thinking, *I left because you hit me. You hurt me*. He was appalled by her reaction. But as her words echoed in his mind and he felt the pain in her voice, guilt started to creep in. *I didn't throw you away. I didn't mean to hurt you. I'm sorry*. He found himself vacillating between anger and remorse, trapped in yet another unresolvable conflict.

Hoping to calm his spiraling thoughts, Arben stepped outside, thinking the fresh air would offer some relief. Instead, the noise from a nearby construction site assaulted his ears, forcing him to cover them. He twisted and turned, trying to escape the blitzing sound, but found no relief.

Among the painful noise, the voice of a jackhammer emerged, taunting him: "Took. Took. Took. Took. Took."

Panicked, he rushed back toward the door but froze when he heard the clear voice of the power saw cut through, it's mechanical whine forming a single, chilling word: "Lliis-s-s-s-s-sseeennn!"

He uncovered one ear, turning to face the sound, his heart pounding.

The wind roared as the saws and hammers shouted, "Shhhaaaam-m-m-m-eeeee! Stop! Stop! Stop! Stop! Shhhaaaaam-m-m-m-meee! Stop! Stop! Stop! Stop!"

Adding to the construction noise and howling wind, the nearby traffic hissed like a roaring jet engine. The cacophony created by all of those sounds sent Arben further into a panic. It felt like a seething, angry mob screaming at him.

His mind raced, intertwining the chaotic voices all around with his mother's hateful words: *Bad karma. Answer to God. He will punish you.* "Shhhaaaam-m-m-m-eee! Stop! Stop! Stop! Stop," the voices persisted, pushing him closer to the edge of despair.

The mental chaos intensified, as every haunting sound from his past seemed to surface at once—the bullies' fists striking him, Benny's belt snapping through the loops before lashing his skin, Arlene's anguished cry upon finding her lifeless sister, and the cruel laughter of classmates mocking him in school.

He clamped his hand over his exposed ear and flew inside, slamming the sliding glass door shut behind him. His breathing was ragged as he wandered aimlessly around the den, rattled and trembling.

Moments later, Tova returned, unaware of the tumult that had just unfolded. "You ready?" she asked, as it was time to leave.

Arben managed to control his heavy breathing, but the look

on his face revealed his distress.

"What's wrong?" she asked.

"I talked to Mom."

He didn't mention the terrifying episode outside; the chaotic voices were still ringing in his ears.

"What happened?" she asked, her concern evident.

He recounted their conversation as Tova placed a comforting hand on his arm. "I'm sorry, Arben. I know you love her."

She hugged him, then stepped back once she felt him relax. Arben had experienced very little physical contact throughout his life, so her embrace and soothing voice helped ease his anxiety.

"You ready for the road?" she asked.

Arben took a deep breath. "Okay."

Twenty-Five

Tarrant County Mental Health Services Center

Wednesday 8:30 am

Dr. Hoffman, eager to clear Arben's case off his desk, started the first of two sessions early on Wednesday morning.

Arben lay on the bed, staring at the ceiling, his empty breakfast tray near to the door. When Dr. Hoffman entered, Arben sat up abruptly, turning his head sharply with his hands clamped over his ears until the door was shut.

"Good morning, Mr. Davis, I'm Dr. Hoffman." The doctor pulled a chair next to the bed and extended his hand to Arben. "May I call you Arben?"

Arben nodded slightly, adjusting to sit on the edge of the bed.

"This shouldn't take long," Dr. Hoffman assured, clicking a pen pulled from his pocket—a habit that instantly grated on Arben's nerves. He flipped open a manilla file, sticking to his old-school preference for real paper and pen over electronic devices.

"Now, Mr. Davis—Arben—I understand you've been hearing voices for quite some time."

Arben remained silent, already disliking Dr. Hoffman. He sensed he was just another doctor who would pretend to care but ultimately offer no help.

"My colleague, Dr. Cruz, noted that these *voices* you've been hearing are most prevalent in the backyard of your childhood home."

Dr. Hoffman paused, waiting for Arben to respond, but Arben remained silent and expressionless.

"I also understand you're an only child."

Arben furrowed his brow, unfamiliar with that term.

"Was anyone else living in your house besides you and your parents?"

Arben shook his head, but suddenly said, "Aunt Crystal, for a while."

Dr. Hoffman clicked his pen a few times before jotting down a quick note.

"Did you get along with Aunt Crystal?"

Arben shrugged, the incessant pen clicking distracting and irritating him.

"Did you ever disagree or get into arguments with her?"

"When she played Dad's piano."

"Hmm," the doctor noted. "And you being a pianist, I suppose you didn't like that?"

Arben didn't appreciate the doctor's indifference and somewhat flippant attitude. He certainly didn't want to engage in a lengthy conversation, but he reminded himself that the more he cooperated, the sooner the annoying doctor would leave. He answered the question with a nod.

"Did she ever try to hurt you or did you ever try to hurt her?"

Arben immediately shook his head, feeling insulted by the question. He'd experienced the pain of violence firsthand and would never inflict it on another living thing.

"But it made you mad when she played your father's piano?"

Arben shrugged, and gave a slight nod.

Dr. Hoffman glanced at his notes. "I see here that Ms. Delgado, Crystal, your mother's sister, lived with your family until her passing."

Arben again gave a slight nod as he began thinking about Aunt Crystal.

"Other than the incident with her playing your father's piano, did you two get along?"

The memory of Aunt Crystal and her friend mistreating his father's piano brought back the anger Arben had felt at the time, but it also sent him on a journey through their past.

Twenty-Six

Arben's childhood home, Austin, Texas

5 years earlier

Just days after Crystal Delgado, Arlene's sister, moved in with Arben and Arlene, Arben returned home from school to a startling scene in the den. Crystal and a strange man were drinking heavily and smoking with abandon. The stranger was at the piano—Arben's late father's piano—which deserved respect. Initially, Arben suppressed his outrage.

"Hey, Arbs," Crystal slurred. As she walked toward him, she stumbled, spilling beer onto the piano keys.

"Stop!" Arben shouted, rushing to defend the beloved piano.

"Sorry 'bout that, Arbs" Crystal said, attempting to clean the mess with her shirttail.

"This is Dad's piano," Arben indignantly stated. "Only *me* and *him* play it."

The stranger threw his arm around Crystal, causing them both to fall into the piano—knocking the ashtray over and scattering ashes across the keys as they collapsed to the floor.

"Sorry, dude," the stranger slurred. "Say," he said, turning to Crystal. "Let's get you another beer." They flopped around on the floor before picking themselves up.

Once they were gone, Arben tried to suck the ashes from between the keys with a dust-buster. His thoughts were consumed with rage. *This is my stuff. You don't even live here. I wish you'd leave forever.* He knew he was wishing evil, but all he could think was *she deserves it.* He was as mad as he'd ever been.

* * *

Returning to the present where he was sitting in the room with Dr. Hoffman, Arben sighed at the memory. Again, his thoughts drifted to another painful experience courtesy of Crystal.

* * *

Thirteen-year-old Arben sat nervously at the back of the auditorium at Austin High School, waiting for his turn to perform in his first piano recital. It was a big event, with piano teachers from across Austin showcasing their students.

As his time to perform approached, Arben started toward the backstage.

"Arby! Buddy," a voice rang out, loud and unmistakable.

Arben froze, taking a deep breath as Aunt Crystal approached, stumbling and chuckling. Initially, he was pleased to see a familiar face but it quickly turned to dread. Her glassy-eyes, unsteady gait, and the unmistakable smell of alcohol told him everything he needed to know

She fell into Arben for a hug, using him to steady herself.

"Hey buddy. You look great."

Embarrassed by her loud voice and slurred speech, Arben muttered, "C'mon." He led her to an empty seat a few rows behind the audience. He sat beside her and leaned in close, hoping she would keep her voice down.

Crystal swayed in her seat and smiled at a few men who'd turned to glare at her unseemly behavior and revealing dress.

"When're ya up?" she blurted at Arben, drawing a few contemptuous looks.

Frustrated, Arben asked, "Can you pick me up later?"

She playfully swatted his shoulder. "Oh, yeah. I got ya, Arbs. I ain't missin' your turn. Say, who's he?" she asked, lustfully eyeing one of the parents.

I have to get away from her, Arben thought. He quickly stood and said, "I have to play."

"Right on, Arbs." She attempted to rise unsteadily. He quickly helped her sit back down before hurrying away. Her voice followed him as she called out, "Kick ass, Arbs!" He ducked backstage, hiding until it was his turn to perform.

* * *

The memory dissolved, leaving Arben staring blankly at Dr. Hoffman once more. A wave of guilt washed over him as he recalled the dark, unspoken thoughts he had once directed at Aunt Crystal—thoughts that would soon transform into an unbearable weight of remorse he could never shed.

* * *

Crystal had been living with Arben and his mother for six turbulent months when tensions finally boiled over.

Arlene, despite her substance abuse and depression following Benny's death, managed to hold down a job and keep her head above water. Crystal, however, was spiraling further into a destructive cycle fueled by excessive drugs and alcohol.

The breaking point came when Arlene returned home from work to find shards of glass scattered across the bathroom floor. "Aw hell. Crystal!" Arlene cried out as she stepped into the bathroom, glass crunching under her feet. "Crystal!" she shouted again, her anger echoing through the house.

The music abruptly stopped, and Crystal came sloshing in. She plopped down on the closed toilet lid. "What's up?" Crystal slurred, oblivious to the storm brewing in Arlene's eyes.

"Dammit Crystal. There's glass everywhere."

"Oops," she said flippantly. "My bad. I had a friend over and you know, he thought it'd be romantic and all to light some candles and take a bubble bath. I think he dropped his beer. My bad."

"Jesus, Crystal. Arben's right across the hall. And I bet you've known this Don Juan for all of five freakin' minutes 'fore splashin' 'round my tub with him?"

Crystal smirked. "Ha! Wrong. We never made it to the bubble bath. And Arbs wasn't even home yet."

"This is totally uncool," Arlene said, crouching down to pick up pieces of broken glass. She was furious, but yelling at her intoxicated sister was pointless. "Just go pass out and hope you still got a place to live tomorrow."

"Yeah? Well, don't do me any favors. 'Sides, look who's talkin'? You been hammered every day since Benny died, so screw you."

Arlene ignored the remark and continued cleaning up the

glass. "Just go pass out."

Crystal staggered off.

Across the hall, Arben listened from behind his door. *Aunt Crystal should leave forever,* he thought bitterly. *She spilled stuff on Dad's piano. She's always drunk. She should just go away for good.*

Those words would haunt him long after that night.

The next morning, Arben leapt out of bed at the sound of his mother's blood-curdling outcry, "Oh my God!" He ran to Crystal's room where Arlene was cradling the lifeless body of her sister.

Arben stood in the doorway motionless, his eyes wide with shock. His first thought was a desperate attempt to undo his wish from the night before. *I didn't mean it. Please, God, no.*

Arlene's voice joined the mental conversation, further tormenting his thoughts: *You don't ever wish evil on no one. God punishes evil thoughts. That's what your daddy done wrong. That's bad karma. Bad karma. Bad karma!*

Staring at the dead body and his mother wailing, Arben couldn't control his runaway thoughts. *I did it again. First Dad, now Aunt Crystal.* Tears streamed down his face as guilt consumed him.

Twenty-Seven

Tarrant County Mental Health Services Center

Wednesday 9:30 am

The sound of Dr. Hoffman's pen clicking pulled Arben back to the present. He hesitated before speaking, his voice just above a whisper. "I wished she would leave forever."

Dr. Hoffman was curious about Arben's sudden change in tone. "Tell me what you're feeling?"

Arben took a deep breath, looking at the doctor with sadness in his eyes. Somberly, he said, "I was mad. I wanted her to leave. I wished it. I wished evil. God punishes evil thoughts."

"Who told you that?"

"Mom."

"And you wished evil on your aunt Crystal?"

The unresolved conflict in Arben's mind came erupted. "Yes!" he snapped, his voice sharp, his eyes locked on the doctor. "And she died."

Dr. Hoffman calmly clicked his pen a few times and updated his notes. Arben compressed his lips, fighting back the urge to lash out at the doctor for his annoying habit.

In an even, measured tone, Dr. Hoffman said, "I'm sure you've been told that your aunt's death was ruled an accidental overdose. Anger can make us think things we don't truly mean. But your thoughts didn't cause her passing."

Arben's shoulders slumped as he whispered, "But I wished it. I wanted her to go away. And she died."

"Because she played your father's piano?"

Arben nodded. "And because she was drunk at my recital, and made a scary man drive me home. Mom yelled at her all the time for sleeping with strangers and bringing them home. I wanted her to stop and go away. I hated her. I wished evil."

Dr. Hoffman jotted down his impressions: *Superstition, paranoid ideation, social isolation, vivid internal fantasies, delusions of reference.*

"You believe your aunt's death was caused simply because you wished her away?"

Arben started blankly, thinking, *You don't understand—just like everyone else. You won't help*. He pulled his knees up to his chest, signaling withdrawal.

In an effort to halt Arben's downward spiral, Dr. Hoffman paused for a moment, then switched gears. "Let's talk about your musical career. Do you enjoy performing on stage?"

Arben, caught in the throes of an emotional rollercoaster, felt the memory of applause rising in waves after each performance as he slowly pulled out of the darkness. He glanced at Dr. Hoffman and gave a small nod, his face softening.

"Do you ever interact with your fans? Greet them, maybe socialize?"

Arben thought about the friendly faces he had encountered after performing and smiled. "Sometimes they shake my hand. They love me."

Dr. Hoffman observed the shift in Arben's demeanor, making quick notes on the contradictions he noticed: *Emotional responses contrary to Schizoid Personality Disorder (SPD), clear self-awareness, positive social engagement, and significant pleasure from performing—each at odds with SPD's defining characteristics.*

"Was your dad a piano player too?"

"Guitar."

"So, he was a musician like you."

The absurdity of the question caused Arben to snort slightly. "No."

"But I understand he taught you how to play."

"He taught me the notes," Arben conceded, smiling at the ridiculous notion of comparing his father's rudimentary guitar skills to his own highly refined expertise. "He didn't like what I played."

"The piano?"

Arben nodded. "Dad played rock and roll. He and Mom didn't like classical music."

Taking a pause, Dr. Hoffman reflected on Arben's case. Despite Arben's evident inconsistencies with Schizotypal Personality Disorder, Dr. Hoffman believed he could draft a diagnosis in line with his initial impressions. However, his boss, Dr. Campos, had emphasized the importance of defensible conclusions, given the risk of external scrutiny. Without additional evidence to support his assessment, Dr. Hoffman knew his finding could face challenges.

Determined to create conditions that might provoke behaviors consistent with SPD, Dr. Hoffman resolved to schedule a follow-up session.

"What do you say we take a break?"

"Okay," Arben said, hoping he was done with the disinterested doctor.

Dr. Hoffman rose and patted Arben on the shoulder. "Relax and I'll be back after lunch. Don't go anywhere," he said in jest.

Arben smirked. "It's loud out there, so I can't go anywhere."

The doctor nodded knowingly. "No, of course. We'll continue later."

Twenty-Eight

Arben's childhood home, Austin, Texas

5 days earlier

Arben was still eager for his mother to see him perform despite their last phone conversation where Arlene told him he no longer had a place at her house. He had left several voice and text messages, but Arlene never replied.

On the day Arben and Tova were set to leave for Austin, Ms. Railey called Arben to say she was ill and wouldn't be able to attend the performance. Although Arben was disappointed, the thought of seeing his mother kept his spirits high.

Upon arriving in Austin, Tova rented a car and drove Arben to his mother's house. Spotting Arlene's car in the driveway, they assumed she was home, especially since it was the middle of the day.

"Mom works at night," Arben said. "I mean, she used to."

"You want me to go with you?" Tova offered.

Arben shook his head.

Arlene had never met Tova, and though Arben wanted to introduce them, he knew Arlene held several negative misconceptions about their relationship. For now, he decided it was better to postpone their meeting.

"Alright," Tova said. "I'll check in to the hotel and then head to the venue. Call me when you're ready for me to pick you up."

Arben exited the car, nervous but excited about seeing his mother. He tried the doorknob, but it was locked. Tova waited in the car watching him.

After knocking several times without a response, Arben took out the house key he'd been carrying since leaving home. Unlocking the door, he waved for Tova to leave before stepping inside.

"Mom?" he called out, breaking the silence.

He wandered through the house, feeling a sense of familiarity. *Nothing's changed,* he thought as he looked into his bedroom. Everything was exactly as he had left it. It seemed as though she had intentionally left the room untouched, almost as if to silently scold him with, "I ain't cleanin' it." Arben could almost hear her voice echoing in his mind. The thought sent a slight shiver down his spine.

"Mom?" he called again, wondering if she might be sleeping.

He moved cautiously toward her bedroom. The door was open, but the room was empty.

Arben walked into the den, and for the first time realized what a dump it was. The paint was cracked and peeling, the carpet worn and outdated, and the furniture was cheap and deteriorating. Beer cans and pizza boxes were scattered around, bugs crawled among clothes, and empty glasses were stuck to surfaces by rings of condensation. The floor was unvacuumed, and papers and debris were strewn everywhere.

"Mom!" he called out one final time after checking the entire house.

With no sign of her, he returned to the den and sat on the couch, waiting. He expected her to walk through the door any minute, but with her car in the driveway, he couldn't help but wonder where she was. The house was eerily quiet.

Arben's eyes fell on the old rickety piano. He played a few chords but quickly stopped—the tuning sounded far worse than he remembered. Memories of the piano being the source of countless arguments and unhappiness between him and his parents made him nauseous. He returned to the couch and waited.

Before long, Arben grew restless and wandered to the backdoor, staring out at the familiar yard.

He pulled his phone out and called Tova. "She's still not here. I want her to see me play."

"Leave her a note with the address and tell her to come to the show."

Arben considered it but was immediately filled with doubt. *What if she's drunk? What if she's mad and starts yelling at me? I wish she wasn't like that.* He became apprehensive about inviting her at all.

"I need to talk to her first," he said.

"Then leave a note asking her to call. You can send an Uber to pick her up or I can swing by."

"Okay," Arben agreed, still clinging to the hope that she

would want to see him perform.

"I'll pick you up in half an hour," Tova said. "I checked us into the hotel, and I'm almost at the venue now."

"Okay," Arben replied and hung up.

With nothing to do, Arben wandered into the backyard. Standing just outside the door, he felt a blend of familiarity and comfort mixed with a sense of foreboding. This was the place where his innocence and imagination had once flourished, but also where he had spent time sorting through some of the toughest experiences of childhood.

The wind rustled the trees, and Arben heard a familiar voice he hadn't heard in a year, welcoming him home with a soft, "Wiiiissssshhhh."

He smiled and replied, "Wish coming true. I'm playing a lot."

The wishing tree responded with a gentle rustle, as if applauding while repeating, "Wish. Wish. Wish. Wish."

He glanced at the tall weeds surrounding the old rusty swing that stood like an ancient relic. "Eerrriiicccc," he heard it say.

Eric, Arben repeated in his mind with a chuckle. *I thought that was your name.* He took a deep breath, recalling some of the turbulent times, and smiled at how far he had come. Closing his eyes, he listened to the same distant mumbling he had heard for decades. As always, he tried to understand what they were saying, but failed. Yet, the familiar sounds of home comforted him.

He started walking down the path he had carved out over the years of wandering the yard. Though the weeds had filled it in, the trail was still faintly visible. As he soaked in the sounds, the air, and the feelings of home, something among the waist-high weeds caught his attention.

A wave of nausea surged through him as he cautiously approached the dense vegetation near Eric. He froze when he came upon his mother's body, face down and motionless.

What is that? he asked himself, his mind rejecting the reality before him.

"Mom?" he called, but she didn't move. "Mom!" he shouted, dropping to his knees. Desperation took over as he rolled her over. Her eyes were open, lifeless. She had been dead for days.

"Mom!" he cried again, shaking her.

He knew she was gone but couldn't bring himself to accept it. For a long moment, he sat there staring at her, his mind struggling to process what had happened.

Finally, he fumbled for his phone and called Tova.

"I found her in the backyard," he said, his voice hollow. She's dead."

Horrified, Tova pulled her car to the side of the road. "Arben, go back inside and call the police. I'll be there as soon as I can."

"Okay," he replied, mindlessly hanging up and dialing 911.

Twenty-Nine

Tarrant County Mental Health Services Center

Wednesday 9:00 am

From the moment Dr. Andrews encountered Arben, he found himself captivated by the unusual nature of the case. Driven by a desire to investigate further, he knew the only way to make time was by extending his already packed schedule—starting his days earlier and ending them later.

He arrived at the office ahead of his colleagues, catching up on overdue paperwork before picking up the phone to call Tova Rawlins, the woman responsible for Arben's commitment. He introduced himself and apologized for interrupting her morning.

"That's quite alright," Tova said. "I'm actually glad you called. I haven't been sleeping well since all of this started, and I'm eager for an update. How is Arben?"

"To be honest, I haven't seen him since he arrived. I'll be talking with him later."

"Will you let him know I miss him?"

"Of course. Now, I've spoken with Marianne Railey, his piano teacher, and she's been very insightful. I understand Arben had a challenging childhood."

"To say the least. Marianne can tell you a lot more about his past than I can, but Arben has shared bits and pieces with me."

"You were the one who arranged for Arben's commitment to this facility. What made you believe he needed professional help? Was it his suicide attempt, or were there other warning signs."

"He didn't try to kill himself," she snapped. "It was the social worker or psychologist—whoever was at the hospital that day—who insisted that Arben needed a formal evaluation." Her irritation mounted. "He and that… that ER doctor jumped straight to labeling Arben as crazy. I told them they were totally out of…" She stopped herself, realizing she was venting. "Sorry."

"That's quite alright," Dr. Andrews said. Not wanting to further agitate her, he added, "Let's set that aside for now. How often did you see Arben in the last few years?"

"We met during the Cliburn competition last year. I was a screener and met him backstage about an hour before his performance."

"My colleague mentioned that the Cliburn is an elite competition."

"It is one of the most competitive in the world. And while Arben didn't make it past the first round, he's as good as any pianist out there—if not better."

"Are you part of the music industry?"

She chuckled lightly. "Not at all. I have a minor in music,

but my degree is actually in communications. I was planning on going to law school before Arben asked me to help him find a gig. Honestly, I'd never done anything like that before, but I knew Arben was a rare talent in need of support. At first, I thought I could maybe help him find a party or something, you know, give him an in and let him take it from there. My husband and I attend several events each year around Dallas/Ft. Worth, and we've heard plenty of pianists who aren't nearly as talented as Arben. As soon as I sent out his demo, my phone didn't stop ringing. Everyone wanted him."

"Sounds like you were surprised."

"Floored. I had no idea how in-demand he would become."

"So Arben went from a handful of performances to playing what, weekly, a few times a month?"

"Within a month of that first gig, he was booked solid every weekend. Within three months, we were traveling constantly with Arben playing three, four, sometimes five shows a week."

"And how long did that go on before the incident in Austin?"

"Almost a year."

"A year on the road," Dr. Andrews said. "That had to be exhausting."

"We took a few days off here and there, but yes, it was."

"How did Arben handle the rigors of performing night after night, and traveling?"

"At first, he handled it great. But as time went on, it started to wear on him."

Dr. Andrews made notes, wondering how much of Arben's issues stemmed from being overworked. "How so?" he asked.

"He was tired and, at times, irritable," Tova explained. "But it was the incident at the Atlanta airport that made me realize he desperately needed a break."

Thirty

Tarrant County Mental Health Services Center

Wednesday 1:30 pm

Dr. Hoffman returned to Arben's room after lunch to continue their discussion. Arben, having finished his meal, sat on the edge of the bed, while the doctor settled into a nearby chair, a folder in one hand, and his ballpoint pen clicking rhythmically in the other.

"Arben, I want you to tell me about the voices you heard—or still hear."

You won't understand, Arben thought. "I want to go home," he said.

"Yes, of course. I understand," Dr. Hoffman replied, dismissing Arben's request.

Their exchange was interrupted by a knock at the door. Dr. Hoffman rose from his chair. "I hope you don't mind, but I ordered you a little dessert."

Tyrell stuck his head in and handed Dr. Hoffman a bowl of ice cream. With a warm smile, the doctor passed it to Arben. "Do you like ice cream?"

Arben nodded. Ice cream sounded great.

As Arben dug into the ice cream, Dr. Hoffman returned to his seat and resumed his questioning.

"The voices, Arben. Are they the same as the loud noise you heard this morning in Dr. Andrews's office?"

Engrossed in the ice cream, Arben barely looked up. "No one ever hears what I hear," he replied, offering his usual response to questions about the voices.

"The loud noises and the voices?" the doctor prompted.

"And the mumbling," Arben added.

"Mumbling?" the doctor repeated. "Like someone speaking softly?"

Arben nodded, finishing the last spoonful of ice cream.

Dr. Hoffman knew it wouldn't take long for the medication mixed into the ice cream to take effect. "So, only you heard the voices, the loud noises, and the mumbling. Did you tell anyone about the voices, maybe a friend at school?"

"They made fun of me."

"Your classmates?"

Arben gave a slow nod, his movements sluggish as a glazed, detached expression settled over him. His thought seemed to drift, his mind slipping into neutral.

"Okay, Arben. Other than making fun of you, did anyone in school ever hurt you?"

"Virgil," Arben murmured.

A wave of warmth and comfort swept through him, unaware it was the medication taking effect. Relaxing further, he shifted further onto the bed, leaning back against the wall. He stared at the doctor as his foggy, drug-induced thoughts coalesced into words.

Lunging forward, Arben's voice rang out with unexpected force. "No!" he shouted, startling Dr. Hoffman. "He hit me and his friends kicked me." He hesitated, the intensity in his eyes fading into a faraway, detached stare. In a quieter tone, he added, "No one stopped it. No one did anything."

"Did you run?" the doctor asked. "Did you tell someone? Did this happen more than once?"

The memory of that day remained vivid in Arben's mind. He recalled being a graduating senior, starting his morning before classes. As he entered the stairwell, he encountered Virgil—his long-time tormentor. Virgil, a dropout notorious for harassing vulnerable students and stealing from the school, had been a source of misery for Arben for years, shoving him and hurling cruel insults.

That morning, the smell of alcohol on Virgil's breath was unmistakable as he stood inches away, jabbing Arben in the chest while spewing threats and insults. Without warning, Virgil punched Arben in the stomach, leaving him gasping for air.

"I couldn't breathe," Arben said to the doctor as the images played through his mind. "People walked by. No one helped."

The image of himself lying in the stairwell, injured and humiliated, resurfaced with painful clarity. He remembered the sting of isolation as classmates passed by, some even stepping over him, Arben picked himself off the floor, disgusted by their indifference.

Arben returned his focus to Dr. Hoffman and repeated softly, "No one helped. I went home."

"What did your mother say?"

Arben sighed deeply, his shoulders slumping. "She said I probably caused it. I had bad karma. The devil in me."

"So, when Virgil hit you, no one intervened, and your mother blamed *you*?"

Arben smirked, his expression showing disappointment.

"Did you often get in trouble with your mother?"

Arben let out another heavy sigh. "God punishes those who wish evil."

As the medication began to cloud his thoughts, Arben's mind raced, fragments of guilt and self-blame surfacing uncontrollably. "God doesn't like stupid. Dreaming is meaningless. Evil thoughts kill people. I killed Aunt Crystal. I killed Dad. I abandoned Mom and she died," he muttered, his words spilling out in a disjointed stream.

"Arben," the doctor gently said. "You didn't kill them. Remember, we talked about that earlier when we discussed your aunt Crystal."

Arben's head wobbled in a slow, unsteady nod. "I wished Aunt Crystal would go away. I wished Dad would go and I abandoned Mom. They all died."

It was clear that Arben was experiencing side effects from the medication. Dr. Hoffman was considering taking a break when a knock at the door interrupted his thoughts.

Dr. Cruz peeked into the room and said, "Doctor, I have the lab results."

Dr. Hoffman nodded, rising from his seat. "Arben, take it easy for a moment. I'll be back shortly." With that, he stepped into the hallway to discuss the results with Dr. Cruz.

Thirty-One

Tarrant County Mental Health Services Center

Wednesday 2:00 pm

Dr. Hoffman stepped into the hallway where Dr. Cruz was waiting with a file in her hand.

"You asked for the lab results as soon as they were ready," Dr. Cruz said, handing him the folder.

Dr. Hoffman took the file and quickly zeroed in on several numbers. "Hmm. I expected elevated thyroid levels or signs of a hormone imbalance, but these figures are only mildly elevated."

Dr. Cruz remained silent, nodding slightly as Dr. Hoffman continued his analysis.

"No evidence of illicit drugs or alcohol abuse. Ah," he said, excitedly. "Slightly elevated white count and CRT levels. These are indicators of stress and often correlate with psychological disorders."

"Sir, those numbers need to be significantly higher to draw a correlation."

Dr. Hoffman slapped the folder shut and handed it back to her. "No single indicator is conclusive, but these findings strengthen my diagnosis when viewed in totality."

"Perhaps, we should—"

"Not now, doctor," Dr. Hoffman interrupted. "I need to complete my interview with Mr. Davis before the medication wears off."

Returning to Arben's room, Dr. Hoffman settled back into his chair, opened his notes, ready to continue. He glanced at Arben, recalling his erratic behavior from earlier. With a steady tone, he asked, "How are you feeling?"

Arben shrugged slightly, still clouded by the effects of the medication. Though foggy and unfocused, the moments of quiet helped him relax.

Dr. Hoffman decided to steer the conversation away from Arben's distressing delusions about the death of his parents and aunt. "We were discussing what happened when you got in trouble with your parents. Can you tell me about that?"

"They sent me to the backyard."

Dr. Hoffman glanced quickly at Arben's file, a note about the backyard catching his attention. "Ah, yes," he said. "That's where you talked to the trees and birds, isn't it?"

This time, Arben didn't deflect as he often did. Instead, his voice took on an almost playful tone, stretching each vowel as though savoring the memories rushing through his mind. "Wissshhhhh. Lissssten. Shesss sessses. Stoooorrrrrm. Flooooood."

The word "flood" jumped out at Dr. Hoffman, the note in Arben's file flashing in his mind—Benny's death by drowning.

Subconscious connection? he wondered.

"When did you hear the voices say storm and flood?"

Arben went still for a moment, staring at the doctor with a puzzled look. "Flooooooddddddd," he repeated with a chuckle.

"Stay with me, Arben," Dr. Hoffman urged, placing his hand on Arben's arm, hoping to guide his attention back to the present. "The storms and the flood, Arben. What happened when the storms came? When the flood began?"

The question triggered more fragmented memories from the day Arben wished evil on Benny. The medication had put him in such a state that he was narrating his vivid mental images while engaging in a verbal Q&A with the doctor.

"Dad was mad, and I wanted to practice. He hit Mom. Birds… Mumbling… I couldn't understand. The trees wishing, and lots of wind. A loud voice like thunder. 'Sstttoorrrmmmmm.' It was loud."

Arben bobbed and swayed, twisted and turned as he told the story. Unconsciously, he patted his pocket, searching for the familiar comfort of the cotton balls he often carried.

"I heard 'Ffffff llll u-u-u-u-u-d-d-d.' I saw rain far away."

"Were you alone the whole time?" Dr. Hoffman asked, watching Arben carefully.

Arben nodded absently, his gaze distant and unfocused.

"So, you went inside?"

Arben slowly shook his head. "Dad's inside. He's mad."

After a moment of silence, Arben squinted and repeated what he was seeing in his own mind. "I wish you would go away."

He broke from his distant stare and focused on the doctor. "I wished evil. Ccrra-a-a-a-a-aiin-n-n-n-n. Nnnnnooooooo. And the trees… The wishing trees. 'Wish! Wish! Wish! Wish!' And Eric. Eric said, 'Eeeeeeevvllllll!'

Arben's features were all over the place, smiling, grimacing, gritting his teeth, eyes swimming, and jerking his head to one side for no apparent reason.

With Arben spinning out of control, the doctor put his hand on Arben's shoulder and said, "Arben. Stop. Take a break."

Arben's spiraling eyes began to slow and regain focus. He steadied himself and gave the doctor a bewildered look, as if slowly waking from a disturbing dream.

"Who is Eric?" the doctor asked.

"The swing set."

The doctor gave him a puzzled look before clicking his pen a few times and updating his notes. *Voices and departure from reality. Abnormal facial expressions, abnormal perceptions, schizophrenia and dissociative disorder, either/or both. Text book SPD.*

Having everything he needed, Dr. Hoffman began wrapping up the interview.

"Arben, I'm sorry for making you relive those troubling memories. But you understand that difficult times eventually end and things return to normal, just like that storm."

Arben spoke matter-of-factly, his voice devoid of emotion. "The storm kept going. Mom and Dad kept fighting. Mom went to the hospital and Dad drowned."

Dr. Hoffman felt a flicker of regret but knew he had gathered everything necessary to complete his assessment—and defend his conclusions, if necessary. "I'm sorry for what you've been through.

You didn't deserve any of it, and you should *never* believe that you caused bad things to happen to *anyone*. That's why we're going to do our best to fix you."

Arben smirked, his droopy eyes blinking slowly. "I can't be fixed."

Dr. Hoffman flashed a confident grin. "Let me be the judge of that."

Arben snorted and stretched out on the bed. He stared at the ceiling through a few long blinks before nodding off.

Thirty-Two

Tarrant County Mental Health Services Center

Wednesday 9:30 am

While speaking with Dr. Andrews, Tova mentioned an incident involving Arben that occurred at the Atlanta airport—a pivotal moment that convinced her he needed a break.

"What happened?" Dr. Andrews asked.

"We'd been on a long run on the road," Tova began, "and we were sitting in the Atlanta airport when Arben suddenly shouted, 'Stop!' He clapped his hands over his ears, so I knew he was hearing something."

"He'd heard things before?"

"A few times."

"Did you hear what he heard in Atlanta?"

"No, but I pulled out a pair of earplugs."

"And that solved his problem?"

"I wish," Tova said. "He refused to wear earplugs. He always carried cotton balls, which is what he put in his ears in Atlanta."

Dr. Andrews remembered Arben mentioning cotton balls the day before when he had to be sedated. Suddenly, it made sense.

"I'd never seen him act like that," Tova said. "We'd been going really hard—airports, rental cars, hotels, driving, late-night snacking—so I knew he needed a break. We both did."

"And the cotton balls did the trick?"

"I guess," Tova replied with a small shrug.

"How long ago was that?"

"About 10 days before we went to Austin, so a little over two weeks ago."

"So you knew something was wrong before… the incident in Austin?"

"Yes and no. Like I said, I thought he was just exhausted before Austin. But you've got to understand, Arben is gifted but odd. Understanding his gifts helps explain why he's odd. When I met him at the Cliburn competition, we stepped outside the concert hall at TCU for some fresh air. Out of the blue, he said 'F sharp.' I said, 'I don't hear any music.' The door to the venue was closed, and we were too far away to hear the performer on stage. He pointed into the distance and repeated, 'F sharp.'"

"What was he talking about?"

"The church bell over a mile away."

"I don't understand."

"The bell was chiming an F-sharp note. I can't confirm he was correct, but I'd bet money he was. He did the same thing many times. He'd tell you what note the fluorescent light was buzzing, a bird was chirping, he even identified the pitch an electric saw was making when we drove past a construction site."

"Exceptional hearing," Dr. Andrews murmured, recalling what he'd read in Arben's file.

"Exceptional is an understatement."

"But it explains why loud sound are painful for him. Has he ever talked about hearing voices?"

She hesitated, worried that her words might be used to help the doctors declare Arben mentally ill.

"When we first met, Arben let it slip about the voices he heard in his backyard. At first, I thought he was just an eccentric musician—not crazy, just… well… odd. I've met a lot of creative people who struggle with social norms, so when Arben told me he heard voices in his backyard, I thought it was just another oddity that came with his extreme creativity."

"And now?"

"Now, I don't know what to think. He's not crazy. Please don't judge him until you spend some time with him. From what I can tell, he had a tough upbringing."

Tova took a deep breath and continued.

"When Arben was little—five, six, seven, I'm not exactly sure—his parents would send him into the backyard after beating him. I think it was a regular occurrence. Again, I don't have any proof, but he has scars. Anyway, he told me that's where he found what he called his only friends. He said he talked to the trees and the birds and other things. He said he could hear and understand what they were saying?"

"Do you think he believed they were real?"

"The voices *were* real, no doubt. But did he believe they were like people or beings? I don't know. I'm sure Marianne told you he's very private and closed off. I tried several times to get him to tell me about his parents. We spent hours together driving to and from gigs, and each time I only got little bits and pieces."

She paused to gather her thoughts. "I learned that his dad was a bar musician, and his mother misquoted the Bible in ways that are hard to imagine. Or maybe she just didn't understand what she was reading. I got the impression that both his parents were pretty far into drugs and alcohol, so it's hard to tell what they actually believed and what came out from the drugs and alcohol. Either way, Arben heard some really crazy things growing up."

Her tone softened, "Early on, I realized something important—Arben might sometimes sound slow or, for lack of a better word, dumb. But the truth is, he's incredibly smart."

"And you believe his parents were abusive? Physically and mentally?"

"I never met them," Tova admitted, "and Marianne can tell you a lot more. But with all the bizarre scripture misquotes, his ideas about God punishing evil thoughts, his reluctance to bad-mouth his parents, and..." she paused, taking a deep breath. "The scars on his legs, back and arms... I hate to think about what he went through."

"Of course," Dr. Andrews said solemnly. "Emotional abuse can leave wounds that are deeper and longer-lasting than physical ones."

Tova's voice wavered. "I don't how anyone could... Arben's mother told him he has the devil in him. Who says that to their child? Arben believed—believes—that bad thoughts bring God's wrath. I'm sure you already know that he thinks he caused his parents' and aunts' deaths because of what his mother taught him. So, yeah, mental, emotional, whatever you want to call it—she messed him up. And physically… One time, when he was changing for a gig, he saw me looking at a scar on his back. It broke my heart when he softly said, 'Dad's belt.'"

She paused, overcome by the thought of Arben's torturous childhood.

"It sounds like he's tough."

"He's a fragile artist," she snapped. "That hardly makes him tough."

"No, I mean he's a survivor. After all the abuse, he still performs what I can only assume is beautiful music."

"Oh, it's beyond beautiful. And you're right. Arben seems to take it all in stride—until these noises finally wore him down."

"Wore him down? You think his problem is fatigue?" Dr. Andrews asked.

"I don't know. But he was handling everything until what you call the incident."

"Let's talk about that. You were there."

Tova inhaled deeply, dreading a trip through one of the worst days of her life.

Thirty-Three

Arben's childhood home, Austin, Texas

5 days earlier

Within thirty minutes of Arben finding his deceased mother face down in the backyard, medical personnel were on-site, documenting the body while law enforcement searched the property and house for clues.

Arben was numb as he quietly sat under the tree where he'd spent his youth. When Tova arrived, she rushed to the backyard and sat down beside him. "I'm so sorry. Are you okay?" she asked, putting an arm around his shoulder.

"I did it," Arben stated unemotionally.

His words were shocking, but Tova remained calm. "I know it hurts."

Arben was staring off into space as he mumbled, "Mom said evil thoughts cause lyin', stealin', and murder."

"What?" Tova said. "No, Arben, that's not what happened."

"Mom said listen, but I didn't. She said God punishes evil thoughts. I did it. I did it to Dad and I did it to Aunt Crystal. I did it."

Tova nervously looked around at the cops, not wanting the officers to overhear what sounded like a murder confession. She leaned closer, her voice softened but carried a firm resolve. "No Arben. You did not do this."

His eyes turned slowly to Tova and, with an unexpected burst of energy, he pulled sharply away from her. His voice rose, filled with anger. "I wished evil. Mom said God punishes evil thoughts. God told Phillip to beware of evildoers, and then He punished them—just like He punished me. I wished evil and she died… just like Dad and Aunt Crystal."

Confused and trying to make sense of Arben's words, Tova thought, *Philippians? God punished the Philistines.* She shook her head, clearing her confusion and snapping back into the moment. She wrapped her arms tightly around him.

"Arben," she said softly and sincerely. "You know that's not true. You didn't cause any of that."

He stared at her, lost in his own grief, anger, and confusion. Tova knew he was beyond rational thinking, so she simply said, "It's going to be alright."

Suddenly, Arben's head turned sharply as the trees hissed and the old swing creaked loudly. He looked around, wide-eyed and rapidly becoming unhinged. "They're laughing at me!"

Tova desperately wanted to comfort Arben but had no idea how. She stroked his hand. "Let's get out of here."

She stood, ready to lead him away, but Arben remained

seated. He released a huge sigh as his head drooped and tears filled his eyes. "I did this," he whispered. "I abandoned her."

Tova sat down beside him as a gust of wind rustled the leaves in the trees. Arben looked up when he heard the blowing leaves say, "Liisssssssseennnn."

"I'm listening!" cried Arben.

As the branches scraped against the house, Arben heard them say, "Wish. Wish. Wish. Wish." The creaking swing joined in, groaning, "Hheeeeaarrrr," while the leaves blasted through with a haunting, "Liiissssseeennn!"

"I'm listening!" Arben screamed, leaping to his feet in a fit of desperation. "I'm listening! I'm listening! I'm listening!" His frantic cries drew everyone's attention.

An on-scene social worker cautiously approached Tova. "Is he alright?"

"He just lost his mother," Tova replied defensively. "What do you think?"

The social worker nodded sympathetically. "You should take him away from here."

"I'm trying."

The social worker crouched down next to Arben. "Mr. Davis," she began softly, "I know this is a difficult time."

Arben turned sharply to her. Initially, Tova thought he was going to explode with anger. He clenched his jaw and stared at the social worker for a moment before swiftly turning away from her and growling, "No!"

Undeterred, the social worker placed a light hand on Arben's shoulder, and he immediately jerked his body away from her.

Nearby, an investigator who had been observing the tense interaction stepped forward and extended a hand to Arben. "C'mon, son," he said in a calm, steady voice.

Arben hesitated, studying the man's outstretched hand. To Tova's surprise, he reached for it and allowed himself to be helped up. Tova immediately slipped an arm around Arben and started them walking. Arben didn't object but shuffled along, his head bowed, mumbling, "The wicked are strange. Liars, taken from their mothers. Wicked. Mom taken. Liars. I wished evil. I didn't listen. I'm sorry. I'm sorry. Mom… Mom… I'm sorry." They slowly moved away from the scene.

Tova drove them to the hotel in silence.

An hour later, Arben was composed as if nothing had happened. He was also eerily quiet as he calmly put on a tuxedo for the evening's performance. Tova, however, had no doubt that he was in denial over his mother's passing. She studied him closely, feeling a growing unease.

An hour earlier, he'd been unraveled, inconsolable. Now he was calm and unaffected.

She grabbed her phone from the counter and started for the door. "I'm going to get some ice," she announced. She exited the room, walking down the hallway as she dialed her husband's number.

Once on the line, she recounted everything. "What should I do?" she asked, her voice tinged with desperation.

David, her husband, sighed heavily on the other end. "Honey, I don't know. It sounds like he's having a nervous breakdown."

"That's what I thought. Maybe he does this when he's stressed.

I just don't know what to do. I wish he had a friend or someone who could tell me if they've ever seen him like this."

"What about his piano teacher?"

"Yes. I've talked with her before. I'll call you back."

Tova immediately dialed Ms. Railey and again explained the situation.

"Oh my," Ms. Railey said. "His relationship with his mother was always turbulent." She shared her observations about Arlene's harsh ways and how she would weaponized scripture to control and punish Arben.

"I've heard him say similar things," Tova said. "Has he ever had a mental episode or anything like this before?"

"Not that I remember. He tends to keep everything bottled up. That's always worried me."

"I wish you were going to be there tonight."

"So do I, but I'm afraid I'm contagious. Please keep me updated."

Tova ended the call with Mr. Railey feeling no closer to a solution. As she returned to the hotel room, she found Arben standing calmly in front of the mirror adjusting his tuxedo.

Glancing at her watch, Tova spoke decisively. "I'm going to cancel tonight. I don't think you're up to it."

"No!"

"Arben," she said gently, stepping closer. "You need time to process what happened."

"No! I'm playing."

"I don't think that's a good idea," she said gently, placing a compassionate hand on his shoulder. "You've been through a very traumatic event. You need time to process everything."

"No! I *need* to play. It helps me."

She wanted to object, but his calm demeaner and apparent clarity left her uncertain. Despite her overwhelming apprehension, she set her concerns aside and drove them to the venue.

Thirty-Four

Tarrant County Mental Health Services Center

Wednesday 11:00 am

Dr. Andrews had been gathering background information by phone from Tova for nearly an hour, carefully piecing together the threads of Arben's story. Finally, it was time to hear about the day Arben nearly drowned in Lake Austin.

Taking a deep breath, Tova began to recount one of the worst days of her life. "In short," she began, "he was performing at a party on the shores of Lake Austin, heard voices, and jumped in the lake."

As the words left her mouth, she paused, overcome by a wave of emotions. "I'm sorry. That was an awful day. It's hard for me talk about."

"Take your time," Dr. Andrews reassured her gently.

"He didn't attempt suicide," she said firmly.

"Tell me what happened and what you think was going

through his mind at the time."

"I don't know what he was thinking. As I said, he's very private. And after it happened, he became even quieter, like he was… I don't know, lost or something. I can't imagine…" Her voice trailed off as she became immersed in the memory, struggling to make sense of that day.

"Anyway, earlier that day, he found his mother face down in the backyard, dead. He was completely devastated and half out of his mind, claiming he'd killed her because he wished evil on her. She'd been dead for a few days, so the body was…" Her voice broke and she hesitated, swallowing hard at the vivid, gruesome memory. "It was like something out of a horror movie. I almost threw up. I got Arben out of there as quickly as I could and took him back to the hotel."

She paused, taking a deep breath before continuing. "I never imagined he'd want to perform after something like that, but a few hours later, he started getting dressed. When I told him I was canceling the performance, he insisted on playing, said he *needed* to play. And, honestly, he seemed perfectly lucid and in control. I've seen him depressed before, and normally he played with even more emotion, which was fine. I thought he would use the performance to work through his emotions. That's what a lot of artists do."

"And he was still fine when you drove him to the venue?"

"He was fine," Tova confirmed. "We barely made it on time, and he started playing almost immediately. Oh my gosh, the way he played brought tears to everyone's eyes. He started with Tchaikovsky's Valse Sentimentale, a really sad, haunting piece. Then he moved on to Lacrimosa from Mozart's Requiem. It was unlike anything I've ever heard—utterly heart-wrenching. From where I was sitting, I could see tears streaming down his face as he poured his soul into the music. But I noticed he kept glancing around, like something was bothering him. Then, suddenly, his eyes widened, and he abruptly stopped playing. He stood up, shouted, 'Fire, run!' and just bolted."

She paused, her mind replaying the unsettling images. "It didn't seem real. I was completely stunned. It took me a moment to even react. By the time I did, he had already run off the stage and into the lake. I screamed for someone to help. And well, you probably know the rest."

"He just ran into the lake? No pause, no dive, no hesitation?"

She thought for a moment. "No. He ran, like he was running away from something. I don't even think he realized he was running into the lake."

"Why do you say that?"

"He doesn't know how to swim."

"How do you know that?"

"He told me about the day he nearly drowned."

"Really? I'd like to hear that."

"Growing up, there was a park with a pool near his house. Arben told me he'd never been in the pool before, but some little girl encouraged him to jump in. As Arben put it, 'It looked fun. If she could swim so could I.' He started in the shallow end, but when he waded into deeper water, his feet slipped out from under him, and he went under. I think he panicked until someone grabbed his shirt, dragged him back to safety, and stood him up. Apparently, he was coughing up water badly, but no one did anything. That was a common theme with Arben—no one did anything. He was beat up by bullies in school, and no one intervened. He had hearing problems, and no one helped. He told me that over and over—'no one helped.'"

Her voice quivered. "When he ran into the lake, that same memory came rushing back to me. I saw him flailing in the water for a few seconds before disappearing under the surface."

"Then someone from the event pulled him out?"

"Thankfully. I don't know who actually pulled him out of the water, but there was a doctor there who gave him mouth-to-mouth right away."

"What happened after they got him breathing?"

"It was scary. He coughed a few times—not as much as I thought he would—but then he just lay there, staring blankly at the sky. Physically, he seemed fine, but mentally… he was somewhere else, completely detached. Despondent, even. I'm not sure what the right word is. He stayed that way until the hospital staff interviewed him the next day. That's when they said he needed to be committed for a 3-day evaluation."

"And that was a week or so ago?"

"A week ago Saturday. I took him back to Ft. Worth to stay at my husband's and my house, and then I drove him to the mental health center Tuesday morning."

"Your husband?"

"Yes, David. He's gotten to know Arben too, though he travels a lot for business, so he doesn't see either of us much."

Dr. Andrews checked his watch, then glanced at Tova's signature on Arben's intake form. "I see you're listed as the person who had him committed. The form lists you as Arben's wife. Any explanation for that?"

She hesitated, embarrassed. "Here's the thing. I haven't known Arben very long, but he means the world to me. When he was in the ER, they said only immediate family could see him. So, when the receptionist assumed I was his wife, I didn't correct her. I know it was wrong, and I'm sorry, but and I couldn't just leave him there alone. He doesn't have anyone else."

"I understand. We'll keep that just between us."

"Thank you. I don't believe in lying, but I'd do anything to help Arben."

"And I'm glad you did what you had to do. But listen, I've got to cut this conversation short. Can I call you later if I have more questions?"

"Of course. And please, do whatever you can to bring him back."

Thirty-Five

Tarrant County Mental Health Services Center

Wednesday 3:30 pm

Dr. Andrews finished rounds with the new doctor ahead of schedule, giving him the chance to join his colleagues for a quick discussion about Arben's case over a late-afternoon snack.

"I've completed my evaluation of Mr. Davis," Dr. Hoffman said.

"Let me guess, you're going to recommend institutionalization," Dr. Andrews remarked disdainfully.

"He's textbook SPD. Supernatural and superstitious beliefs, paranoid ideation, a history of abuse, drug addicted parents, guilt-fueled delusions, and, of course, auditory hallucinations. Honestly, Stan, I'd be negligent if I didn't recommend treatment."

Dr. Cruz chimed in. "I have to agree with Dr. Hoffman. My own assessment of Mr. Davis leads me to the same conclusion. Furthermore, I've documented instances of aggressive behavior and symptoms indicative of dissociative disorder."

"Both of you are forming conclusions based entirely on interviews. He's in a strange place after suffering some of the worst days of his troubled life," Dr. Andrews remarked. "I don't think you're seeing the full picture."

Dr. Hoffman snorted. "Good lord, Stan. The young man's problem started in childhood. He genuinely believes he killed his parents. Frankly, I'm amazed he's held it together this long."

Dr. Cruz nodded in agreement. "The last thing we need is for Mr. Davis to spiral out of control and shoot up a movie theater full of innocent people."

Dr. Andrews raised an eyebrow, chuckling dryly. "Seriously? Shooting up a theater? I've seen nothing in his background—or otherwise—that suggests he's ever been violent or even remotely aggressive."

"It's there," Dr. Cruz insisted. "He may hide it well, but I can sense the rage simmering just below the surface."

Dr. Andrews smirked. "*Sensing* rage is hardly scientific."

The remark irritated the young doctor. "I thought you read the hospital report," Dr. Cruz fired back. "He punched a wall and bloodied his hands after his suicide attempt. Is that scientific enough for you?"

Dr. Andrews clicked through the file, his expression neutral as he scanned the details. "If you read the entire report," he began, "you'll see that *that* episode occurred just hours after Arben discovered his mother's body in the backyard of his childhood home—not because he's harboring violent tendencies. If finding your mother's decaying body isn't grounds for an emotional outburst, I don't know what is. And, by the way, there's no mention of bloodying his hands. As I said, it's prudent that we consider Mr. Davis's complete profile before making any recommendations."

Dr. Cruz snidely said, "Doctor, the facts are clear. This young man has endured a lifetime of abuse. His parents beat him with a belt. He was bullied and ridiculed in school. He witnessed his father beat his mother repeatedly. His socioeconomic status likely led to poor nutrition, and I strongly suspect prenatal exposure to illicit narcotics. All of the these are recognized causal factors of SPD. I stand by my conclusions. He's a ticking time bomb, and it's only a matter of time before he goes off. He's certainly not going to get better on his own."

Dr. Hoffman added, "And let's be honest. In today's climate, I'm not going to risk my professional reputation, my license, or even my freedom. The public and judicial system are quick to hold us accountable for failing to prevent Mr. Davis from committing an act of violence."

Dr. Andrews shook his head, disappointed in his colleagues. "We took an oath to do no harm."

Dr. Hoffman scoffed. "Cry me a river, Stan. That oath includes protecting the public. We'd be negligent if we allowed this young man the opportunity to unleash his pent-up rage on an unsuspecting public."

"More speculation," Dr. Andrews countered. "There is no solid evidence of *any* pent-up rage, nor is there a precedent for violent behavior in his history." He paused, taking in a deep, calming breath before adopting a conciliatory tone. "Doctors, I've spoken with two people who know Arben well—his piano teacher, who has known him since childhood, and the woman who has traveled with him every day for the past year. Both describe him as a sweet, gentle soul. In my opinion, he's less likely to become violent than any of us."

"Do I need to have you committed, Stan," Dr. Hoffman joked.

"I'm serious, Will. Hold your diagnosis until I finish the background and get a chance to sit down with him."

Reluctantly, Drs. Hoffman and Cruz agreed, but Dr. Hoffman warned, "Just so we're clear, Stan, I'm not sticking my neck out on this one. The kid has all the signs of serious emotional and cognitive impairment. If you manage to convince Dr. Campos otherwise, you and he will be on your own. I'll hold my report until tomorrow afternoon, but I will not change my diagnosis nor my recommendation."

Dr. Cruz stepped toward the door, pausing to add, "I suggest you give him a sedative before interviewing him. He can be volatile. And, with his insistence on keeping the door closed, I recommend stationing Tyrell outside the door in case he turns violent. I did."

Dr. Andrews found the suggestion overly dramatic, but rather than engage in a fruitless argument, he simply said, "Thank you."

"He won't need anything today," Dr. Hoffman interjected. "I gave him a quarter milligram of clonazepam earlier. He's probably out."

Glancing at his watch, Dr. Andrews said, "I'll see him first thing in the morning."

Thirty-Six

Tarrant County Mental Health Services Center

Thursday 8:00 am

Dr. Andrews arrived at his desk early and promptly dialed Marianne Railey.

"Good morning," he began. "I'm sorry to call so early. Is this a good time?"

"Yes, of course," Marianne replied. "I'm sorry about yesterday."

"No need for that. But I do have a few more questions, if you have the time."

"Fire away."

"You said for a time Arben lived with you. Can you walk me through what happened that led him to leaving home?"

"Arben called me one night, distraught, asking if he could live with me. It was obvious he'd been in a fight with his mother. Now, the last thing I wanted was to get in the middle of a family squabble, but when Arben said, 'she hit me,' I agreed to pick him up. When he got in my car an hour or so later, I could see the bruise forming on his face."

"Did his mother object to his leaving?"

"I don't think she even knew he had left. Arben was silent during the first half of the drive, but then suddenly erupted. 'She hit me! I didn't do anything!' His emotions were all over the place—angry, sad, hurt, disillusioned, and depressed. He let everything out, and I just listened."

"I'd like to hear what he said, if you can."

Marianne's tone was resolute, but there was a trace of anger. "I can. It wasn't that long ago. Arben had just returned from the Cliburn competition, the biggest achievement of his life. That's where he met Tova. Arben was thrilled that she had taken a professional interest in him. You know she's married, of course. Anyway, Arben's mother accused him of being immoral and evil for sleeping with Tova."

"Which he hadn't," Dr. Andrews quickly added.

"Of course not. But Arlene was convinced Tova was some sort of harlot—again, not true. Nonetheless, Arlene constantly badgered and insulted Arben, calling him and Tova every unkind name she could think of."

"Any physical violence?"

Softly, Marianne replied, "I think so."

She paused for a moment before continuing in her normal voice. "I'm fairly certain Arlene struggled with drugs and alcohol. Arben mentioned more than once that the school had sent letters home due to his excessive absences. He wasn't skipping school. He stayed home because he was afraid she was so intoxicated she might die if he wasn't there."

She went silent, shaking her head in disgust.

"Did he tell you that?"

"He would say, 'Mom's sick.' But Arben never really *told* me anything directly. I went to their house once, and it left an impression I won't forget. Arlene was sprawled on the couch—her hair tangled, eyes red and droopy, surrounded by empty pill and liquor bottles. I was appalled by the conditions Arben was living in, but I kept that to myself. As I was about to leave, Arlene said to Arben, 'Ain't many days pass without you backtalkin' me or actin' like the devil." Marianne let out a bitter grunt in disgust at the injustice.

"Was Arben a defiant or disobedient child?"

"Never. That's the point. Arben was the sweetest little boy, but everyone has their limits. I seriously doubt Arben ever backtalked her. He probably tried to defend himself. And to accuse him of 'acting like the devil'? I'll never forget her saying that. I wanted to grab him and march him right out of there, never letting her mistreat him again."

"But of course, you couldn't. Tell me about the ride to your house after he left home."

"Oh, sorry," Marianne said with small sheepish laugh. "I got a little off track. Back to the day he moved in. Arlene was mad about him making friends with Tova, so he'd been trying to avoid her. He got up early that day—before sunup—to grab a quick breakfast and hide out until she left for work."

"She was a waitress?"

"I got the impression she changed jobs frequently. Quit, got fired, I don't know. Anyway, early that morning Arben ran into his mother and a stranger she'd brought home the night before."

"Was that a regular occurrence?"

"I don't think so. And I believe Arben had a problem with anyone replacing his father. He tried to ignore the stranger, which apparently made Arlene mad. Maybe she was still drunk from the night before or on something, but Arben made some remark that infuriated her, and she punched him."

"And I'm sure Arben didn't fight back."

"Of course not, but doctor, something snapped in Arben that morning."

"Snapped how?"

"I'm sure Arben had been on the receiving end of his parents' violence many times, but when he was telling me all this, he seemed to zone out when he got to the part about her hitting him. His thoughts were all over the place—like he was reliving more than his mother hitting him. Some of it made sense like 'she hit me' and 'I didn't do anything,' but then he mumbled things that didn't make sense: 'the belt,' 'mean,' 'bullies,' and a name: Virgil. It was like he was trapped in his own memories, reliving all the pain and mistreatment he'd endured."

"Did he say anything more about the incident with his mother?"

"Not a word. But when we got to my house, he sat at my piano and played for over an hour straight. I think he was working through it at the piano."

"Sounds like he told you more than you thought."

She chuckled. "I guess he did. That was such an awful day

for him. But over the years, I guess he's shared enough fragments of his life that I've been able to piece them together. Thank you for listening. I don't know why, but I feel better."

Dr. Andrews smiled. "You're welcome. I appreciate your candor. This conversation will undoubtedly help. Like you said, it's not any *one* thing. You have some pieces, I have some, and Tova has some. Hopefully, between all of us, we'll arrive at a solution."

"God willing," she said. "And thank you for caring."

"And you too."

Thirty-Seven

Tarrant County Mental Health Services Center

Thursday 9:30 am

After speaking with Marianne Railey, Dr. Andrews took a few minutes to review his notes. There were many issues bothering him, but with limited time, he couldn't chase every idea.

Grabbing his tablet, he made his way to Arben's room. As he entered, Dr. Andrews quickly shut the door behind him. Arben was sitting on the bed, finishing his breakfast.

"Arben," Dr. Andrews began, "I don't know if you remember me. I was the first doctor you met when you arrived on Tuesday."

Arben set his tray on the desk beside the bed and gave the doctor a hard look. The memory was clear, causing Arben to unconsciously rub his shoulder where the doctor had forcefully jabbed him with a hypodermic needle. A feeling of contempt swelled within him.

Dr. Andrews offered an awkward smile. "That's right. I was

the one who gave you the shot. I am sorry, but it was for you own good."

Arben wasn't ready to forgive. He studied Dr. Andrews with distrusting eyes. "I want to go home."

"I know. But let's chat for a while, okay?"

Arben gave no response.

"Let me just start by saying I'm *not* going to give you a shot. I'm just here to talk."

Arben maintained an expressionless stare.

"I spoke with Marianne Railey and Tova Rawlins, and they tell me you're a gifted musician."

"Ms. Railey," Arben corrected.

Dr. Andrews settled into the solitary chair while Arben's eyes followed him closely.

"Ms. Railey," he acknowledged. "How about we talk about music?"

Arben wasn't interested in talking to another disingenuous doctor, but again reminded himself that talking to them was his only way out. "Okay."

"Ms. Railey and Tova said you like to rewrite classical pieces. How long have you been making your own version?"

"Always."

Dr. Andrews could see that Arben was being deliberately obstinate. "Listen, I know you're tired of all this and ready to go home."

Arben nodded without expression.

"And I won't make promises I can't keep. I'm not here to tell you I can fix everything or magically make your life better."

Arben furrowed his brow, unsure of what to make of the doctor's honesty. This was something new.

"Okay," Arben said cautiously with a look and tone that said, 'go on.'

"I've read your file, talked with Ms. Railey and Tova, and learned all I can. But now I want to hear from you."

"Okay," Arben repeated, his guarded stance softening slightly. There was something about Dr. Andrews' straightforwardness that intrigued him. Still, skepticism lingered, reinforced by the memory of the unsettling encounter with Dr. Hoffman. Arben didn't know what had left him so disoriented, and while the possibility of being drugged hadn't crossed his mind, he knew something wasn't right.

Now, facing Dr. Andrews, Arben braced for the usual routine. This doctor had already jabbed him with a needle, and Arben felt convinced he would eventually conclude the same thing as the others: *exceptional hearing*. He'd heard it before—from the doctor at the free clinic and the school nurse. His mother had dismissed his condition outright, calling it nonsense, among other things.

However, Dr. Andrews' admission—that he couldn't guarantee anything—made Arben pause.

After a brief staring match, Dr. Andrews crossed his legs and casually said, "Ms. Railey and Tova said you've been hearing voices for many years."

"I already talked about that."

Dr. Andrews flashed a warm, friendly smile. "I know. And like I said earlier, this might lead nowhere. I can't promise anything beyond listening and hoping to uncover something that leads to a solution—or at least an explanation."

"Exceptional hearing," Arben stated after hearing the word explanation.

Dr. Andrews nodded. "You've heard that said to you often, haven't you?"

Arben nodded solemnly.

"I think that's *part* of the problem," Dr. Andrews said. "But there's something missing. Let's figure it out together. Tell me, how long have you been hearing voices?"

Arben found Dr. Andrew's honesty intriguing. "Always," he replied.

"Always?"

Arben nodded.

"Okay. Do the voices sound like me, like you, or like someone in particular?"

Arben furrowed his brow. He had never been asked that question before. With the exception of Olivia, this was the first time Arben felt like someone genuinely believed him.

As his distrust and skepticism began to dissolve, Arben lowered his guard, wanting to help the doctor understand what he had lived with his entire life.

He gave the question some thought, and a feeling of enlightenment came over him. He'd never considered what the voices sounded like. "Like voices. Different," he said. "Some sound normal. Some are low, some soft, some mumble. Birds sometime sing; other times, they talk."

"That's fascinating," Dr. Andrews remarked. "Are all of them different?"

Arben nodded, his mind cycling through the mental archive

of unseen voices. "Sort of. Some sound the same when I hear them again."

"When did they start saying things like fire was coming?"

Arben went silent, trying to remember when he'd first heard the word 'fire.'

"Like a year. Maybe longer?" the doctor prompted.

Arben shook his head. "I never heard 'fire' until Austin. But the rest since before I met my friend Olivia."

The doctor glanced down at Dr. Cruz's report: *Childhood friend.* "Do you remember how old you were when you met Olivia?"

Arben shrugged. "Second grade."

"That's more than ten years," Dr. Andrews remarked, a touch of astonishment in his voice. "In all those years, how often have you heard voices?"

"Always."

"You hear them every day?"

Arben nodded.

"But you don't respond or talk to them?"

At that, Arben's discomfort returned as memories flooded back—vivid and unwelcome—of the first time he'd told someone that he talked to the voices.

Thirty-Eight

Langdon Preschool/Arben's backyard, Austin, Texas

14 years earlier

On Arben's his first day of kindergarten, he approached a trio of tough neighborhood kids on the playground, eager to make new friends.

"I talk to trees," Arben announced with a bright smile.

One streetwise six-year-old scoffed. "What's wrong with you? Are you stupid?" The remark drew snickers from his fellow toughs.

Unfazed, Arben's grin widened. "I listen to birds talking too," he added, further confusing the young thugs.

"Man, dude's a weirdo," one of the kids declared, prompting a high-five from his friend and a chorus of laughter from onlookers. The boy gave Arben a shove. "You a freak."

Arben got the message and sulked away while the laughter continued.

* * *

Later that same day, Arben sat in his weed-riddled backyard surrounded by rusted car parts, worn-out tires, broken appliances, and Eric—the creaky, forgotten swing set.

"Why don't they like me?" he asked into the silence. "They don't even know me."

The wind blew through the trees, and a voice replied, "Wwwiiiissssshhhh."

Arben listened carefully and turned as a bird perched in an old dead tree added, "Talk. Talk. Talk. Talk."

"I talked," Arben said. "But they laughed at me."

"Wwwwiiiiisssssshhhh," the tree repeated.

Arben's gaze dropped to the ground as he sighed. "I wish they were my friends."

He traced idle patterns in the dirt with his finger, losing himself in thought. The laughter from earlier still lingered in his mind as he wondered what made him different—and why it had pushed others away.

Thirty-Nine

Tarrant County Mental Health Services Center

Thursday 10:00 am

Dr. Andrews observed quietly as Arben withdrew into his own thoughts. When Arben finally looked up, he chose not to share the memory of his first day of kindergarten.

"Did the voices talk back to you," Dr. Andrews repeated.

Arben shifted uncomfortably in his seat. "We already talked about that."

Dr. Andrews smiled. "We'll come back to that. Do you realize you've been hearing voices for over ten years, and you're a professional musician?"

Arben nodded, puzzled by the remark.

"You're an impressive young man."

Arben smiled, but his confusion deepened. "You never heard me play."

The doctor chuckled. "I mean, you're remarkable for thriving where many others might not. Despite the voices, loud noises, and everything else you've endured, you've become a concert pianist. That's impressive. I look forward to hearing you play, maybe later."

Arben enjoyed hearing his life described as impressive. For him, it had always felt like a few shining moments peeking out of a mostly difficult and painful existence.

"I enjoyed talking with Tova and Ms. Railey. They're looking forward to your return to performing."

Arben's cheerful demeanor suddenly faltered.

"Isn't that what you want?" Dr. Andrews asked, noticing Arben's sudden glumness.

Arben shrugged. "I messed up."

"Because of what happened at the lake in Austin?"

He nodded, thinking, *they won't want me to perform anymore.*

"Let's not talk about that yet," Dr. Andrews suggested. "I want to hear more about the voices and the loudness."

"We already talked about that," Arben said, sinking further into despondency.

"C'mon, Arben," Dr. Andrews said with a smile, playfully jabbing Arben in the leg. "You're doing good. Let's keep going. Just tell me, are the voices loud?"

"No," Arben said, trying to shake off the gloom for Dr. Andrews' sake.

"So, the voices and the loud noise are separate things. You don't hear loud voices or loud sounds that start talking, do you?"

Arben thought for a moment, then shook his head. "The sound gets loud, not the voices."

"Okay, that's helpful. It sounds like they're separate issues, but there must be a connection between them. Let's talk about when you were little and first started hearing them. I understand your father played guitar."

"Dad didn't like classical music or piano playing. He said the best way to stop a piano player is to take the music away. But I don't need the music."

Dr. Andrews smiled at the joke, then a question struck him.

"Did your parents ever tell you why they named you Arben?"

Arben's expression darkened. "Mom was Arlene and Dad was Ben. Ar Ben. They made fun of me in school."

"I think it's a unique and special name. Some people have nothing better to do than to ridicule those who are better than them."

Arben's face lit up. "Better?" he repeated, confused. To him, being different had always meant not as good.

"Absolutely. You're a gifted musician. How many people can say they can play like you?"

Arben's mood lifted as Dr. Andrews paused to consider what he had learned.

He wondered if Arben was suffering from a significant mental illness. He ran through the terms he'd been trained to use when describing mental illness: *voices, violence, high-functioning, delusional?* It would be easy to make a textbook diagnosis based on those criteria alone.

Then, he considered a second set of variables running though his mind: *physical and emotional abuse, highly creative and intelligent, neglect.* Those were patterns he had seen many times in depressed individuals and adolescents acting out. *Perhaps it's simple mental exhaustion, not illness or impairment,* he told himself.

Recognizing the conflicting symptoms, Dr. Andrews realized the need for further questioning and analysis, but time was running out.

"Arben, let's take a break. I'll have them bring you lunch a little early, and we can talk again later. Does that sound good to you?"

Arben nodded. For the first time, he found himself looking forward to another conversation with a doctor.

Dr. Andrews stood and gave him a reassuring pat on the shoulder. "See you after lunch."

Once Dr. Andrews left, Arben began sifting through a new wave of thoughts. *He believes me.* The realization felt foreign to him. He wanted to have hope—something he hadn't dared to feel in years. *Maybe he can fix me.*

That hope pulled him back to the question he had been asking for years: *What is wrong with me?* He had always seen himself as broken. But now, something new struck him—Dr. Andrews hadn't said *exceptional hearing,* the dreaded term always followed with, *there's nothing we can do.*

Intrigued, Arben allowed himself to consider the possibility. *Maybe they can fix it,* he wondered, the idea of being normal—an idea he had abandoned long ago. However, his hope dimmed as he recalled Dr. Andrews admitting that he might not be able to help.

Forty

Tarrant County Mental Health Services Center

Thursday noon

Intrigued by Arben and sensing a missing piece, Dr. Andrews skipped lunch to study Arben's case file.

With less than 24 hours before Arben's voluntary commitment would expire—leading to either his release or indefinite detainment—Dr. Andrews felt the pressure mounting.

Sitting at his desk, he couldn't shake the thought of Arben's extraordinary hearing. *All of his problems revolve around his hearing*, Dr. Andrews mused, poring over the details in the file.

Acting on a hunch, Dr. Andrews headed to his car. An avid marksman, he had a pair of passive headphones stored in the trunk. He retrieved them and made his way to Arben's room.

Handing the headphones to Arben, Dr. Andrews explained, "These aren't for listening to music. They're used by hunters and marksmen and are known as passive ear protection. They block out almost all sounds, much like earplugs."

Arben immediately remarked, "I don't like earplugs. I can't hear anything, and I feel pressure in my head."

"Try these instead. They'll block the sound but they won't make you feel pressure," Dr. Andrews offered, slipping the headphones over Arben's ears.

As Arben's skeptical expression shifted to one of surprise, he shouted, "I don't hear anything!"

Dr. Andrews nodded, signaling for Arben to stand and walk toward the door leading to the hallway. However, as Dr. Andrews reached for the doorknob, Arben hesitated, his eyes wide with alarm, and began to back away.

"It's okay," Dr. Andrews assured him.

"What?" Arben said, looking puzzled.

Dr. Andrews gently pulled the headphones away from Arben's head and said, "Trust me. It won't be loud."

Reluctantly, Arben said, "Okay."

Dr. Andrews placed the headphones back on Arben's head and reached for the doorknob again. Arben inhaled sharply, fearing the worst as the door opened. His expression shifted to one of bewilderment.

"I don't hear anything!" he shouted.

Together, they walked down the hall and back.

Once they were back in Arben's room with the door closed, Dr. Andrews removed the headphones and asked, "Did you hear any loud noises or voices?"

Arben shook his head and walked to the window to glance out at the courtyard.

"That's great. That proves the sounds aren't originating inside your head. Let's go back to the voices. Are they always outside?"

Arben nodded and pointed at the door. "Out there."

"I thought you only heard loud noises."

Arben shook his head. "Mumbling."

"You hear them outside this room?"

"I hear them now."

"Really? Even with the door closed?"

Arben nodded.

"What do they sound like?"

"Talking."

"Talking?" Dr. Andrews repeated. "Like two people talking or a single voice?"

"Talking. Like a lot of people talking at the same time."

"Just conversation?"

Arben nodded and said, "Mumbling."

The doctor jotted down a few notes. "When you *do* understand what they're saying, do they ever tell you what to do?"

Arben looked puzzled as he thought about the question, again glancing out the window while he pondered. He had never had this conversation with anyone before, and it felt good to finally talk about it without fear of being ridiculed or dismissed.

"We talk," Arben said. "They say things like 'listen' and 'wish,' and other things."

"Have they ever told you to steal money, push someone down, or to *do* anything?"

The question took Arben by surprise and irritated him. He quickly responded, "No. They said rain. They said listen. They said fire."

"You heard the word fire in Austin before you went in the water."

Arben nodded, looking away and feeling shameful. Again, he glanced out the window.

"I want to hear about that day," Dr. Andrews said, hoping to learn about the moments before Arben allegedly tried to commit suicide.

However, Dr. Andrews glanced at his watch and remembered his scheduled meeting with Tova.

"But I tell you what. Why don't you relax for an hour. I'll have them bring you a snack or some food. I have a meeting, but I'll be back in an hour."

He hurried out of the room to his office.

Forty-One

Tarrant County Mental Health Services Center

Thursday 2:00 pm

After his session with Arben, Dr. Andrews rushed into his office, where Tova was already seated, waiting patiently.

"Sorry for keeping you. And thank you for stopping by, though it really wasn't necessary. I do have a few questions, but they could've been handled over the phone."

"I know, but I was hoping to see Arben. Plus, I brought you some videos of his performances." She pulled a thumb drive from her purse and handed it to Dr. Andrews.

"Thank you. This could be helpful, and I'm sure Arben would love to see you. He's a very unusual case. There are a lot of perplexing things about him, and I don't want to jump to a diagnosis without a thorough investigation. It's difficult to do that in only three days."

"What are you suggesting?" Tova asked, sensing there was

more to his words.

"I'd really like thirty days."

She shook her head. "Oh, I don't know. What did he say? I think he'd go crazy unless… Can he can have a keyboard to play?"

"Probably, but let me be frank. My colleagues believe he has a significant mental impairment. They interviewed him and think the voices he hears, his lack of social skills, and the recent breakdown all support their diagnosis. And, honestly, it's hard to dispute their findings."

Tova took a deep breath and was about to disagree when Dr. Andrew added, "but I believe they're wrong."

"They are," she quickly agreed. "Like I told you on the phone, Arben's different but he's not crazy."

"The problem is, I'm one against two. Upon his release, we may be required to file an official assessment with the State, which becomes part of a permanent record. Arben could be adversely affected by the wrong diagnosis. But more importantly, I'd like to figure out exactly what's going on."

"You think that's possible?"

"Ordinarily, I would say no, but there is something about this case that makes think there's an identifiable underlying cause."

"Which is why if you don't release him, you don't have to file a diagnosis right away?"

"Exactly. It gives me time to find the truth. The challenge I'm facing is convincing my colleagues that while Arben is eccentric, his recent struggles or *condition*, if you will, could simply be the result of fatigue or stress."

"And if you can't convince them?"

"A diagnosis of a mental disorder isn't the end of the world, but the stigma associated with it could interfere with his long-term recovery."

"You still think he needs long-term care?"

"There's no doubt that Arben has been through a lot in his short life. I think he's done a remarkable job in coping, but he is struggling."

"He is," Tova agreed. "And I told him he needed to talk to someone. He didn't want to come here, but I told him he'd feel better and hopefully get better."

"Everyone needs to unburden themselves at times. And for someone like Arben who's been mistreated, lied to, manipulated, bullied, and forced to endure all the other difficulties he's experienced without a support system, therapy is crucial."

"But you said you agree with me that he's not crazy."

Dr. Andrews smiled. "That's not a diagnostic term, but I agree with your sentiment. However, Arben is carrying a lot of emotional baggage that will take time to unpack. I don't think he needs institutionalization."

"What then?"

"Counseling. I've already seen how just listening to Arben tell his story has helped. He needs more of that—a lot more."

Tova felt relieved. "So, like meeting with someone like you every week and talking through all the crap he's been through, from his abusive parents to all the things you mentioned?"

Dr. Andrews nodded. "But first, we need to make absolutely sure there isn't an underlying medical or mental condition at play. And we must be cautious not to assign a diagnosis that could weigh him down further."

"So, you want another thirty days to figure it out?"

"Maybe less. I'd like you to help me convince him to stay."

"Can I see him?"

"Absolutely."

As they walked down the same halls Arben had walked two day earlier, Tova was shocked by the distant, echoing cries of patients—the same haunting sounds that Arben had found disturbing.

The moment she entered Arben's room, he jumped up. "Tova!"

He moved to hug her but stopped just short, standing close and smiling at her. They had become good friends, but Arben never initiated physical contact.

She put her arms out and gave him a warm hug. "How are you?" she asked.

The hug gave him a great feeling of comfort. "I want to go home."

"I know." She paused, searching for the right words to convince him to extend his stay. There was no easy way to put it, and she felt certain he would refuse. Finally, she blurted, "They want you to stay a little longer."

"No!"

She took his hand with both of hers. "How about just one more week? I can bring you a keyboard. I know you want to practice, and you can play for the doctors."

Arben's face lit up at the idea of performing for the staff, and Tova saw the spark of interest. "Then we'll go back to my house, or you can go to Ms. Railey's."

"I want to go..." he began, his voice trailing off. Tova braced herself, expecting him to dig in his heels, but to her surprise he finished with, "...but I can practice here."

"Good," she said, giving him another hug. "Listen, I have to go, but I'll bring your keyboard and maybe work on booking some gigs."

Forty-Two

Tarrant County Mental Health Services Center

Thursday 2:30 pm

After Tova left, Dr. Andrews returned to his seat by the bed, but noticed Arben's restlessness. He stood up and said, "Let's change things up. Why don't we go outside and get some fresh air?"

Arben glanced at the door with a fearful look. "It's loud out there."

Dr. Andrews held up the headphones. "Not with these," he said with a smile.

Arben slipped the headphones on the allowed Dr. Andrews to guide him outside.

The courtyard outside Arben's room featured a mix of tables, chairs, and a lush green lawn. It was a serene environment where patients and staff could relax.

As the door to the facility clicked shut, Dr. Andrews carefully removed the headphones from Arben's head. "Everything okay?" he asked.

Arben turned his head from side to side, offering a gentle nod and a smile.

"Much better," Dr. Andrews remarked as he and Arben settled into chairs tucked beneath the trees.

Arben was pleased to be outside. He tilted his head slightly, listening to the distant hum of traffic, the rustle of the leaves in the breeze, and the birds chirping from above.

Dr. Andrews noted Arben's raised awareness and said, "Do you hear something?"

Arben nodded. "G-sharp."

Puzzled, Dr. Andrews repeated, "G-sharp?"

Arben pointed at the trees. "G- sharp. G-sharp. F. F. G-sharp," he said, mimicking the rhythm of the bird's song.

"Is that what you hear the bird saying?"

Arben chuckled and shook his head. "No. Notes."

Dr. Andrews smiled. "Ah, I see. G-sharp—like on a piano."

Arben nodded.

"What else do you hear?"

Arben turned and tilted his head, listening closely to the sounds around them. "Wind. Trees. Mumbling."

"Mumbling? From where?"

Arben raised his hand and pointed, but Dr. Andrews only heard the faint noise of traffic, chirping birds, and the gentle rustle of the trees, but no mumbling. He wanted to explore what Arben was hearing further, but time was limited.

"That's remarkable, Arben. And I want to talk more about it, but for now, I need you to tell me about the night you heard the word 'fire.'"

Without hesitation, Arben said, "I was playing. The trees said, 'ffffff.'"

"Okay, who said fire?"

Arben hesitated, unsure of the answer. "A boat was going by, and I heard, 'u-u-u-u-u-n-n-n.'"

Dr. Andrews tried to imagine what Arben was describing. "A motor boat sputtering," he thought out loud. "Arben, I want you to relax and see if you can put yourself back in that moment before you went in the lake. You were sitting at the piano..."

Arben nodded.

"Tova said you were playing Mozart."

"Lacrimosa," Arben confirmed.

"Good. Close your eyes and tell me what was going through your mind."

Arben closed his eyes and took a deep breath. "I was sad." He hesitated, his voice quieter. "Mom was gone. Dad was gone. I don't know."

"Try to focus. Can you hum Lacrimosa?"

Arben tried to hum the music, but his thoughts took him away. "Mom should have been there," he said. "I missed her. The boat, or something."

"What about the boat? Was it talking?"

Arben's memories sharpened, and the words came faster. "More boats puttered down the lake. Ru-u-u-u-n-n-n-n-n!" he exclaimed. "I felt the wind and heard, 'Fffffff.' I was playing Mozart, and I was sad." His eyes remained closed, but his brow began to wrinkle. "Ffffff. Wiiiisssshhhh. Fffffff. R-u-u-u-u-u-n-n-n. The voices—they were distracting me. It made me mad because I was playing."

Suddenly, Arben's eyes flew open. "Fffffiiirrrrrreeeee. R-u-u-u-u-n-n-n-n!" he shouted, looking at Dr. Andrews with fear in his eyes.

"The boats said 'run' and the wind said 'ffff,' but where did the rest come from?" Dr. Andrews asked.

Arben shook his head, just as puzzled as the doctor. "Fire. Run! I heard it," he said firmly. "It wasn't loud like the hum, but I heard it—like a shout. Like when Dad told me to stop playing the piano."

The realization hit Arben all at once. His expression froze, staring at Dr. Andrews with his mouth open.

Dr. Andrews was also astonished, believing they had struck gold. The pieces were suddenly coming together, revealing a deeper truth. *The grief and sorrow Arben had been carrying over his parents' passing*, Dr. Andrews thought. *It had collided with the memories of abuse, neglect, and fear—all converging into a single command: Run.*

Dr. Andrews sensed they were on the brink of a major breakthrough, yet the meaning behind it remained unclear. "You could hear yourself playing Mozart?" he asked.

Arben nodded.

"And you could hear the boat and the wind."

Another nod.

"Everyone else could hear you playing the piano along with the boat and the wind?"

"They don't hear what I hear," Arben replied.

"I understand, but the voices weren't coming from inside your head."

"No. I was thinking. I heard me inside my head."

"Thinking about what you were playing?"

Arben shook his head. "I was thinking about Mom." He took a deep breath and added, "She was supposed to hear me play."

"Did you *want* to jump in the water?"

Baffled by the absurdity of the question, Arben said, "No." His tone firm and sharp.

"Did you want to hurt yourself or…" Dr. Andrews paused, hesitant to ask the most important question of all. "Did you want to kill yourself?"

Arben's eyes widened with surprise. "No!"

"But you jumped in the water."

"I didn't know it was there. I can't swim." His voice suddenly dropped. "I messed up."

Dr. Andrews smiled and placed a reassuring hand on Arben's shoulder, his voice steady and kind. "Arben, you didn't mess up. It's not your fault." He let that sink in for a moment before offering another warm smile. "You're doing great. Give me a minute to document all this."

The silence that followed was filled with the low rumble of distant thunder along with several sporadic gusts of wind. Overhead, the sky darkened with the first hint of rain.

Dr. Andrews noticed Arben shifting uneasily at the changing weather. Rising from his seat, he said, "Let's head back inside. It'll give us a break while we walk." He handed the headphones to Arben as they strolled toward the building.

Forty-Three

Tarrant County Mental Health Services Center

Thursday 3:00 pm

Dr. Andrews escorted Arben back to his room in silence. The walk gave Dr. Andrews time to digest the truth about Arben jumping into the lake. It wasn't a suicide attempt, as he'd been led to believe, but rather an accident. Yet, Arben's complex history still left many unanswered questions, primarily, why was he hearing voices when everyone else merely heard noise?

Once inside the room, Arben took his seat on the edge of the bed while Dr. Andrews settled into the chair.

"Okay," Dr. Andrews said. "Now that I've seen it for myself, I understand when you say no one hears what you hear, and we may never fully understand that. But I believe what you hear is real. I think there are two things happening: the voices and the loud noise. When you arrived in my office earlier, you said the voices were loud. When do normal sounds become too loud for you?"

"I don't know." Arben said, reflecting on those moments when the sounds had unexpectedly become painfully loud. "Outside at Tova's," he added.

"What happened outside Tova's?"

"I had just talked to Mom, and she hung up on me. I was mad, so I went outside for some fresh air. Everything was normal until an explosion hit, like something from a war movie. Everything was loud, rumbling all at once in my head. It was terrible. I covered my ears but it was still too loud."

"What did you do?"

"I shouted stop!" His face bore the fright he had felt that day. He looked off into the distance as the event replayed in his mind. "I ran inside. I told Tova I had called Mom but I didn't tell her about what happened outside."

"Why didn't you tell Tova?"

"We were going on the road. I didn't want to make her mad or worry. I didn't want her to cancel the gigs."

"When you play concerts, Tova mentioned you sometimes twist and turn. Is the applause too loud?"

"Sometimes. It's loud, but it's okay because they like my playing. I turn my head, and it gets better."

"But you don't hear voices?"

Arben shook his head.

"Okay," Dr. Andrews continued, glancing down at his notes. "You heard voices when you first arrived here, at the concert with the fire, and in your backyard?"

Arben nodded as the doctor studied his list of instances when Arben had heard voices.

"So, it seems like you mostly hear them outside, except here, outside your room."

Arben shook his head. "Outside the cafeteria at school," he clarified.

"Right. Outside," Dr. Andrews confirmed.

"No. Outside the cafeteria is *inside* the school, not outside. It's where everyone got snacks."

"You said it was outside the cafeteria. Where were they getting snack from?"

"The vending machines."

"The vending machines," Dr. Andrews repeated, a vague sense of familiarity tugging at him.

"Alright," Dr. Andrews said, quickly adding to his notes. "In your backyard, when was it loud, and when was it just voices? Was it ever both?"

Arben spoke in a somber tone, recalling the last time the backyard sounds were loud. "When Mom died. They kept saying 'listen.'" He fell silent for a moment, allowing the painful memories of that day to resurface. "I heard more voices than normal, but I guess they weren't loud. Just a lot of them at once."

Dr. Andrews noticed the stress and fatigue in Arben's voice. "I understand," he said. "That was a tough day. *This* has been a tough day, but you've done great. Let's take a break."

With that, Dr. Andrews stood and left the room. He stopped just outside Arben's door for a moment, glancing around the quiet, empty hallway. He listened carefully but heard nothing loud or unusual. The source of Arben's discomfort baffled him.

Forty-Four

Tarrant County Mental Health Services Center

Thursday 4:00 pm

Following his session with Arben, Dr. Andrews made his way to the office of Dr. Campos, the hospital administrator. He needed approval to extend Arben's temporary stay at the facility. However, the discussion shifted, with Dr. Andrews focused on persuading Dr. Campos to delay filing the diagnosis submitted by his colleagues.

"Filing a report that characterizes Arben as a danger to himself or others, as my colleagues have suggested, is premature and likely highly inaccurate. He's been through a lot in his short life, but he's never posed a threat to anyone," Dr. Andrews argued.

"Our diagnostic report is not for law enforcement," Dr. Campos replied. "It is simply required reporting, and only under certain circumstances."

"Yes, but it gives the State the power to investigate further.

Please don't subject him to that."

"That is for the State to decide."

"Look, I'm convinced this kid's just got some sort of hearing problem, not a cognitive deficiency. Please don't give the authorities a reason to drag him through the system."

"I read that he has exceptional hearing, but this is the first I've heard of a hearing *problem*," Dr. Campos said, flipping through the file. "I see nothing here about that, only that he's hearing voices."

"That's misleading. Yes, he's hearing voices, but they aren't originating in his head," Dr. Andrews clarified.

"I don't understand. Do *you* hear the voices he's allegedly hearing?"

"No, but—"

"There you go. If he hears them but you don't, they must be inside his head. End of discussion."

"No sir, that's wrong. He hears things other people don't hear."

"Exactly. He's hearing voices."

Dr. Andrews smiled. "I feel like we're doing a comedy routine. Let me be more succinct. Arben has exceptional hearing, as noted in his file. I believe that allows him to hear things with his ears that you and I can't hear."

Skeptically, Dr. Campos said, "That would be a first."

"I agree. This is a very unusual case. I haven't submitted my findings because I haven't quite finished my evaluation, but I believe the underlying problem *is* Mr. Davis's hearing."

"You have proof?"

Dr. Andrews explained his noise-cancelling headphone

experiment, where Arben, who had been unable or unwilling to leave his room, was perfectly fine walking down the hall with the headphones on. "Please, give me more time."

"His three-day commitment ends tomorrow morning. Has he agreed to extend his stay? And does he understand that by staying, he or his insurance carrier will be responsible for the bill? Do we even know if he has insurance or the means to pay?"

"He has agreed to stay, but I don't know his insurance status. I suspect the woman who brought him here would guarantee payment."

"I want confirmation of that." Dr. Campos paused for a moment, considering his options. "Drs. Hoffman and Cruz have already submitted their reports, but I will hold off submitting the final report for forty-eight hours. No more."

"Thank you," Dr. Andrews said, making a beeline for Arben's room.

Forty-Five

Tarrant County Mental Health Services Center

Thursday 4:30 pm

After meeting with Dr. Campos, Dr. Andrews entered Arben's room full of nervous energy. His thoughts churned as he searched for answers. Arben remained seated on the bed, calm in contrast, while Dr. Andrews paced around the room anxiously.

"The issue in the hallway," Dr. Andrews began, "what do you hear?"

"Loud talking."

"Like a room full of people?"

Arben nodded.

"Where?" Dr. Andrews asked.

"The end of the hall. By the door, and there," Arben said, pointing to the right side of the hall.

"Sit tight," Dr. Andrews instructed.

He stepped into the hallway and studied the surroundings.

The hall was empty and quiet. Dr. Andrews stood still, listening carefully. He noticed an air conditioning intake vent above Arben's door with a fan motor making a low, gentle hum. He made note of the sound, then walked down the hall, where three vending machines emitted the low hum of their compressor motors.

Then it clicked. *The vending machines outside the cafeteria—Arben mentioned loud noises at school.* The revelations continued as Dr. Andrews recalled the vending machines in the break room adjacent to the doctor's offices. The pieces were falling into place as he thought back to Arben's initial episode when the overwhelming noise led to his sedation.

Dr. Andrews strolled slowly down the right side of the hall where Arben had pointed. He examined the area, noting nothing but doors, security lights, and cameras. He walked the length of the hall several times and then pressed his ear against the wall, where he heard a low hum. He studied the security lights more closely, detecting a faint buzz that was barely audible. It puzzled him that such weak sounds as the low hum of the transformers and the vending machines, could cause a problem.

Dr. Andrews sent a text message to Carl Jackson, the facilities manager, asking to meet him in the hallway outside Arben's room.

When Carl arrived, he and Dr. Andrews stood looking up at one of the lights mounted above each patient's door.

"Are these lights always on?" Dr. Andrews asked.

Carl pointed to a tiny sensor beneath each light. "They're motion-activated. They trigger when a patient steps outside of his room."

"And the cameras, are they always on?"

"They're also motion-activated as well as infrared. When activated, they track the movement."

"Meaning they move?"

Carl nodded. "And zoom in on the motion while recording."

The doctor stepped back and noticed more sensors on the doors and wall.

"Are they all powered by a single source?"

"There's a series of transformers that run on a single circuit," Carl replied.

"Is it possible to turn them off?"

"We could kill the breaker, but I'd need approval from Dr. Campos for a security bypass."

"I'm on it," Dr. Andrews said, thanking Carl before heading for Dr. Campos's office.

Forty-Six

Tarrant County Mental Health Services Center

Thursday 4:45 pm

Dr. Campos listened skeptically from behind his desk as Dr. Andrews explained his theory about Arben's hearing issue and requested permission to turn off the breakers.

"Absolutely not," Dr. Campos stated. "The security of this institution is not to be compromised for random experiments."

"This is not some random experiment. I know transformers hum, albeit slightly, but this could be part of Arben's problem. I'd like to shut off the security system and soda machines for just a few minutes. Carl said it's just a matter of killing a few breakers, that's all. I can text him to turn the system back on the moment we finish."

Dr. Campos shook his head. "The security system is silent."

"Not completely. The transformers that run the cameras and lights hum. It's possible the problem is the sound the cameras make when the infrared kicks in, or perhaps the sound of the cameras zooming in. I don't know for sure. Or, it could just be the vending machines."

"That's ridiculous."

"Maybe, but sir, he's fine when he wears passive ear protection. As I mentioned earlier, I believe Mr. Davis suffers from some sort of physical malady. While his extraordinarily sensitive hearing, along with his creativity, makes him a bit odd, he's not cognitively deficient or hearing voices in the manner of a schizotypal individual, as my colleagues have attested to in their findings. I believe my experiment will prove what I am saying."

"I read the file. He hears voices. I know you think it's because of his hearing, but there's simply no concrete proof of that. I also consulted with Dr. Hoffman, who cited several additional symptoms that support his diagnosis, along with the lab results. I must follow protocol."

"And drag Arben through an invasive process, interrupting his life and career, only to find out his problems are physical and not psychological?"

"You know how it works."

"You're making a terrible mistake," Dr. Andrews remarked.

"Doctor, don't make me the bad guy. We have processes and procedures for a reason, and if I made an exception for every patient who *could* have a simple earache, this institution would grind to a halt."

Dr. Andrews took a slow deep breath, considering for a moment what he was about to do. He pulled a business card from his pocket and dropped it on Dr. Campos' desk.

"I hate to do this," Dr. Andrews said respectfully. "But I think we've got a problem, sir."

Dr. Campos picked up the card. "What's this?"

"This is his *wife's* business card."

"So?"

"Her last name is Rawlins, not Davis. They're are not married. She's a friend who manages his professional career."

"So?"

"So, the woman who signed the voluntary commitment form didn't have the right to have him admitted. Technically, we've kept Arben here against his will."

Dr. Campos quickly pulled up Arben's file and confirmed the truth. Irritated, he glared at Dr. Andrews. "Who else knows?"

"Only you and I."

After a long silence, Dr. Campos said, "I supposed you want to kill the security system."

"If we shut off everything in the hall that produces a low hum—the vending machines, security lights, and air conditioning—I believe Arben will calmly walk down the hall. Remember, he doesn't know where the loud noise or voices come from, and I'm not going to tell him what we're doing."

"I don't like this, and I don't appreciate being coerced. However, I don't see what choice I have. But I will be there to monitor every move."

"Of course, doctor. Thank you."

Forty-Seven

Tarrant County Mental Health Services Center

Thursday 5:00 pm

Arben sprang to his feet, quickly covering his ears when Drs. Campos and Andrews entered his room, pausing briefly before closing the door.

"Arben," Dr. Andrews said as he approached him. "We have two quick tests for you. First, you're going to walk down the hall without the special headphones."

"No, please!" Arben cried, backing away. "It's too loud."

"Please, Arben," Dr. Andrews urged. "I think it will help."

Arben's breathing grew heavy as dread took hold, his mind anticipating another painful experience.

"Don't you want to figure out what's causing the problem?" Dr. Andrews asked.

Arben studied both doctors for a long moment, reining in his anxiety as he decided that Dr. Andrews' words were enough for him to relent.

He nervously allowed Dr. Andrews to guide him toward the door but winced as they got close.

"The door isn't even open yet," Dr. Campos remarked, his tone carrying reproach.

Dr. Campos pulled the door open sharply, and Arben's reaction was immediate—his body stiffened, and he clamped his hands tightly over his ears.

Dr. Andrews led Arben five steps into the hallway. Arben twisted and turned, clearly distressed even with his hands tightly over his ears. Dr. Andrews gently pulled Arben's hands just a few inches away from his ears.

"Ow! Stop!" Arben cried out, shaking his head violently while twisting and turning, trying to cope with the noise. "Please make it stop!"

He slapped his hands over his ears and ran back into his room, kicking the door closed behind him.

Dr. Andrews stuck his head in the room and said, "You did fine, Arben. Relax for a minute. We'll be right back."

Out of earshot of Arben's enhanced hearing, Dr. Andrews called Carl and put him on speaker with himself and Dr. Campos. Carl stood in front of the breakers that powered the hallway outside of Arben's room, as well as the security system.

"Okay, we're ready," Dr. Andrews said. "Carl, count to ten, then shut off the breakers. Leave them off for two minutes, then switch them back on."

The doctors returned to Arben's room, where he immediately began retreating toward the far wall, fear written in his expression.

Dr. Andrews stepped closer and calmly said, "This is the last test, Arben. We're going to do the same thing."

"No!" Arben shouted, raising his hands to cover his ears. Suddenly, he froze. The panic in his expression melted into confusion. He lowered his hands. "What?" he muttered.

Tilting his head, Arben walked to the door and opened it. "There's nothing," he said, bewildered. Stepping into the dark, silent hallway, he strolled away from his room, smiling.

"It stopped," Arben exclaimed. "They're gone. What happened?"

The doctors watched Arben with astonishment. He was a completely different person—relaxed, happy, and seemingly carefree.

Dr. Andrews looked at his watch with urgency. "Arben, I need you to come back inside quickly."

Arben was almost to the room when he was suddenly struck by an explosive sound that only he heard as the breakers came back on, restoring power to the motion sensors, security lights, and vending machine.

"Ouch!" he cried out, grabbing his ears, rushing into his room, and slamming the door behind him.

Amazed, Dr. Campos looked at his watch. "Two minutes. I've never seen anything like that."

"I'm glad we both saw it with our own eyes," Dr. Andrews remarked.

"He should see an otologist immediately. It's hard to imagine how no one noticed this before."

"I can understand his chemically dependent parents missing

it. And the schools he attended were starved of resources and overwhelmed with violence and drugs. Still, you would have thought someone would have recognized it. He should also see a neurologist. I suspect hearing *that* acute has caused some neurological abnormalities."

Dr. Campos reached out with a smile, shaking Dr. Andrews' hand. "You probably saved this young man from a lifetime of misdiagnosis. He will still need professional counseling, but that can be done on an outpatient basis. I'll amend the report and expedite his discharge papers."

Dr. Campos walked away, and Dr. Andrews returned to Arben's room.

Arben was sitting on the bed wearing an angry expression.

"I'm sorry about that," Dr. Andrews said. "You were supposed to return to your room before the sound resumed. But the good news is, you just proved to everyone that you're actually hearing loud noises."

"So you believe me?" Arben asked, his tone hopeful.

"Absolutely. But I believed you before today."

Arben's face lit up as he felt the weight of the world lift from his shoulders.

"You can fix it?"

"I don't know about that," Dr. Andrews admitted, slightly deflating Arben. "But this is a step in the right direction."

Later that day, Dr. Andrews slipped the passive ear-protecting headphones over Arben's ears and led him to the lobby where Tova was waiting.

Tova greeted Arben with a brief hug before turning to Dr.

Andrews. "So, what was wrong with him?"

"We don't know for sure," Dr. Andrews admitted. "But I was able to demonstrate the link between Arben's hearing and his behavior."

"A link? What does that mean?" Tova asked.

"It means he's not mentally ill."

"But he's not cured either."

Dr. Andrews shook his head. "While his hearing is exceptional, as both of you know, it is that acute hearing that is likely the source of his hearing voices and loud noises."

"So we're back to where we started," Tova said, disappointed.

"Not at all. I'm referring him to a hearing specialist and a neurologist where they can go beyond testing his hearing and see if they can uncover what's *really* going on."

Tova wasn't convinced, but Arben was all smiles. He was excited about being released and full of hope that a lifetime of hearing problems could soon be over. For the first time since Olivia, someone believed him.

"I'll call you later with some names," Dr. Andrews said.

Arben gladly rushed out of the building, eager to return to his life and career.

Forty-Eight

Office of Dr. Raymond Nelson, MD, Otologist

A few days after being released from the Tarrant County Mental Health Services Center, renowned otologist Dr. Raymond Nelson administered an extensive series of hearing tests on Arben. Following the evaluation, Arben and Tova met with Dr. Nelson to discuss the results.

"Young man," Dr. Nelson began, "you have the most developed hearing we've ever tested. It is nearly beyond the capabilities of our equipment to measure. We did, however, detect an unusual sensitivity to low frequencies. But what concerns me more are the anomalies near the tympanic membrane in both ears. They could be acoustic neuromas or a cholesteatomas, although, I have never seen such occurrences in both ears simultaneously. There is also a slight possibility that it could be some form of cancer."

"Cancer?" Tova repeated, her voice filled with fear.

"It is a possibility," Dr. Nelson reiterated.

"What are those other things?" Arben asked. "The neuro thing and cholesta thing?

"Both are noncancerous growths," Dr. Nelson explained. "Cholesteatomas are skin growths that develop in the middle section of the ear. Acoustic neuromas are rare tumors that can form in different parts of the ear."

"And if it's not those, I have cancer?" Arben asked, his concern growing.

The doctor gave a cautionary grin. "Cancer is possible but less likely. Tumors in this area are almost always neuromas and cholesteatomas, which are non-cancerous. However, they typically present with hearing loss and balance problems. You clearly have no hearing loss. Have you experienced any balance problems, dizziness or ringing in your ears?"

Arben shook his head. "I hear loud noises."

"Is it a high-pitched ringing sound?" Dr. Nelson asked.

Arben shook his head again. "A low rumble."

"We don't see that with neuromas."

"Does that mean it's more likely cancer?" Tova asked.

"Cancer can present in many ways," Dr. Nelson said. "It is a possibility, but we will know more after a biopsy. Cancerous tumors in the inner ear are rare, so they could be cysts or some other skin lesion, but I'd rather not speculate." He glanced at Arben's file before continuing. "I see the referring physician, Dr. Andrews, recommended Arben see a neurologist."

"We have an appointment in a few days," Tova said.

"Very good. Normally, I would schedule an MRI for a closer

look at Arben's inner ear and to plan the biopsy, but the neurologist will do that. Who are you seeing?"

"Dr. Carver."

"Dr. Serian Carver? He's the most sought-after neurologist in the country. And you already have an appointment?"

"Yes," Tova confirmed.

"And you can fix it, whatever it is?" Arben asked.

Dr. Nelson's cautionary grin remained as he said, "Depending on what the biopsy tells us, surgery may be the best option."

"And that would fix it?" Arben asked.

"Perhaps, but I'm not a surgeon. Let's first find out what we're looking at."

Tova's mind raced, desperately seeking reassurance that it wasn't cancer. "So it could be something else?"

Dr. Nelson nodded. "It could be a flap of skin or some other innocuous abnormality that has nothing to do with his hearing condition."

Arben's hope dimmed a bit, fearing all this was in vain.

"We will know a lot more after the MRI," Dr. Nelson said.

"Will it hurt?" Arben asked.

"You may feel a little sting from the biopsy, but the MRI is completely painless. You will lie in a tube for thirty minutes while the machine takes pictures." Dr. Nelson paused, realizing a potential issue. "MRI machines are loud, and given your extraordinary hearing, it could present a problem." He jotted down a quick note. "Ordinarily, I don't attend MRI sessions, but your case is so unusual that I'll make sure I'm there to inform the technicians about your unique condition. No need to worry."

Arben, still seeking hope, asked, "But if it *is* one of those… neuro… or cholestral things, you can fix it?"

"Let's just say I'm cautiously optimistic," Dr. Nelson said.

Arben grimaced. After a lifetime of voices, loud noises, ridicule, and family tragedies, he felt his newfound hope of a solution fading away. The room seemed to grow colder as the weight of uncertainty settled over them. Dr. Nelson's words, though intended to provide cautious reassurance, left Arben with a gnawing sense of apprehension.

* * *

Arben lay in bed that evening, his mind finally clear as the medication from the mental health facility had fully left his system. He stared at the ceiling, hoping for a miracle while grappling with the harsh reality that his problem might never go away. *I can't play with earplugs*, he reminded himself.

A bittersweet comfort washed over him as he relived the heartfelt applause he'd received every time he performed. *They love me*. He imagined bowing before a vast audience. On stage, he was somebody—important and loved. Memories of the high school talent show brought back a happy moment when even the abusers and naysayers had changed their opinion of him.

Those cherished memories felt like all that was left of his career. Silently, he wept for a future that seemed unlikely to include performing.

Forty-Nine

Crosby Imaging Center, North Dallas, Texas

Arben checked in at the Crosby Imaging Center and was soon positioned on the table, prepared for his MRI scan. The technician held up a pair of headphones and said, "You'll hear music playing from these, but if the sound from the machine gets too loud, let us know, and we can stop."

He placed the phones over Arben's ears, and Arben smiled as the music began to play.

"Can you still hear me?" the technician asked.

Arben nodded in response.

They turned the machine on, and Arben initially twisted his head slightly. Then he steadied himself and said, "Okay." He was nervous, still thinking the MRI might hurt. He didn't fully trust doctors, but the music helped calm the tension from being inside the intimidating machine.

Just as Arben was beginning to relax, the technician's voice startled him through the headphones, "Please remain as still as possible."

Arben nodded.

Dr. Nelson had briefed the technician earlier about Arben's sensitive hearing and remained in the control room in case he was needed.

The tech turned to Dr. Nelson and said, "You're welcome to wait in the lounge."

Dr. Nelson took the hint and replied, "Of course. I'm meeting several colleagues to review the results. Can you burn them to a disk or put them on a server when you're done?"

"There's no one scheduled after Mr. Davis, so no problem."

As the procedure got underway, Arben tried focusing on the light jazz playing through the headphones, but the clicking and thumping of the machine was unnerving. Trapped in a tube with strange noises was a challenge. He tried to remain still, but an occasional short blast of noise startled him. Each time it happened, it struck him with a gripping fear that the loud sound would continue to the point of pain. The tight quarters added to his anxiety, and he couldn't help but react—wincing and turning his head when the loud noise hit.

Fortunately, it only lasted a split second. The first few times Arben squirmed, the technician reminded him to remain still, forcing Arben to fight through his fear and discomfort. With each blast, he held his breath, remaining still and enduring the brief but painful noise. He never fully relaxed, but by focusing on the music, he managed to remain still throughout the rest of the procedure.

The clicks, thumps, and noise ended, and soon the music stopped.

"That's it," Arben heard the technician say.

The table began moving, and soon Arben was back on his feet. He breathed a huge sigh of relief.

"You did fine," the tech said.

"I'm done?" Arben asked.

"Yes sir. You can head through that door."

Tova was waiting for him with Dr. Andrews.

"How was it?" she asked.

He shrugged. "Okay. Not bad. They said I'm done."

"You remember Dr. Andrews from the facility? He said they will call us later with the results. What do you say we grab a bite to eat?"

Arben and Tova left while Drs. Nelson and Andrews convened in a meeting room equipped with a computer and several large screens for reviewing the results.

"Any word from Dr. Carver?" Dr. Nelson asked.

"He said he would be in the neighborhood around this time, so I expect he'll show up any time. Either way, they will send him the results."

They loaded the MRI images into the computer and were immediately captivated by what they saw. They focused on the anomaly just beyond Arben's eardrum.

Dr. Nelson leaned close to the screen. "The continuity with the surrounding tissue indicates it has been there since birth. However, it's unlike anything I've ever encountered. The texture and contouring are particularly striking. It's not a tumor. Look at the shape. Tumors usually look like masses of tissue, somewhat circular or blob-like. I've never seen one shaped like that."

"Could it be a foreign body?" Dr. Andrews inquired.

"*Behind* the eardrum? How would it get there? No, this is some sort of congenital growth."

"It almost looks like the fins of a vent," Dr. Andrews observed.

Dr. Nelson paused, his expression suddenly enlightened. "Yes, like an air conditioning vent. The striations or fins, if you will, appear uniform. But if you look here," he said, pointing at a section of the screen while cycling through a series of images, "the fins change. They're farther apart in certain scans."

The two doctors continued studying the images until Dr. Carver arrived. Once he entered, Drs. Nelson and Andrews stepped aside, allowing him to take over the computer.

Moments into the review, Dr. Carver angrily said, "This can't be right. This is a standard MRI."

"Yes," Dr. Nelson agreed. "I believe that's correct."

"Dammit! I specifically asked for a functional MRI. I need to see how this young man's brain is functioning." He scowled at the screen and shook his head. "The images are supposed to capture brain activity. This is useless."

He abruptly stood and said, "Reschedule the test at Redelton. Tell them it's for me. They'll put him in tomorrow." He paused for a moment, then turned to Dr. Nelson. "Doctor, let's also conduct a frequency sweep."

"A frequency sweep?" Dr. Nelson questioned.

"Yes. The fMRI will capture his brain activity when he's asked to perform certain tasks. However, I noted in Dr. Andrews' records that Mr. Davis was responding adversely to certain frequencies. As part of the fMRI, let's capture his brain activity when he's subjected to a sweep of all the audible frequencies—20 to 20,000 hertz."

"Okay." Dr. Nelson agreed. "He showed an unusual sensitivity to low frequencies at my office. What do you expect to see?"

"Who knows," Dr. Carver replied. "It may be a waste of time. Mr. Davis's history of hearing voices and loud noises may simply be his exceptional hearing, but I'd still like to capture his neural profile during a hearing test, including a frequency sweep."

Fifty

Redelton Imaging Center, Ft. Worth, Texas

At the Redelton Imaging Center, Arben lay motionless, tuning into the technician's instructions. "Try to relax," the technician advised, holding up a device that resembled a virtual reality headset. "You'll see images in the headset. Do what the screen asks but remain as still as possible. You will also be asked questions."

"No music?" Arben asked.

"Sorry, you'll need to hear the questions and instructions."

"Okay," Arben agreed, a bit apprehensive about the potential noise from the machine.

After slipping the device on Arben, the technician said, "Here we go."

Arben nodded as the table slid him into the tube. Feeling less anxiety than during his previous MRI, he found the headset to be an intriguing distraction. Nonetheless, he took a deep breath, bracing for any potentially painful sounds.

The machine began its familiar clicks and thumps, prompting Arben to take a few more deep breaths, just as he did before each performance on the piano.

Suddenly, an image appeared in the headset: *Squeeze your left hand*, the caption read. Arben complied. The next image said: *Relax your hand*. The third prompt displayed: *Imagine a dog in the park*. Arben thought of Franklin Park near his childhood home, recalling the people walking and playing with their dogs.

The next prompt simply read: *Relax*. The images and instructions continued rapidly, with some asking him to move a finger or wiggle his toes, while others asked him to conjure up images of people, animals, emotions, and landscapes, among other thoughts. Arben found the experience quite engaging. He managed to tune out the machine's clicks and thumps, except for the occasional sharp burst of noise that made him wince. Despite the discomfort, he resisted the urge to twist or turn his head. Much like the previous MRI, the blasts were painful but brief.

The images stopped, and the technician's voice came through the headset. "Arben, you are doing great."

Dr. Nelson then patched in his portable hearing equipment. "Arben, we're going to run a sweep of frequencies. You will hear a very high-pitched sound. Don't worry, it won't be loud. Then we will slowly lower the frequency until it is just a low hum."

"A glissando," Arben remarked.

"Is that a musical term?" the doctor asked.

Arben nodded. "When you slide across all the keys."

Dr. Nelson smiled. "Okay. Glissando. If the sound becomes uncomfortable, try to work through it, but if it becomes unbearable say 'stop.' Okay?"

Arben nodded, and Dr. Nelson added, "And try not to move. Here we go."

The technician restarted the machine, and the familiar clicking and thumping resumed. Arben's headphones filled with a soft, high-pitched sound that slowly descended. As it approached the lowest frequencies, Arben began to squirm and abruptly ripped off the headset.

"Stop!" he shouted.

The technician hurried into the room to remove Arben from the tube. "Are you okay?" he asked.

Arben, though visibly shaken and breathing heavily, nodded.

Dr. Nelson entered and asked, "Was it too loud?"

"Yes."

"Did you hear voices or anything other than sound?" Dr. Nelson asked.

"No voices, but loud mumbling."

Dr. Nelson seemed puzzled by the comment, but turned to the technician. "I think that will suffice."

The tech led Arben back to the waiting room where Tova was anxiously waiting. "Arben did fine," the technician assured Tova. "I've sent the results to Dr. Carver's office."

"Thank you," Tova replied. "Can you tell us what you saw?"

"Let's wait for Dr. Carver to review the results. He's the expert."

Disappointed, Tova nodded. "I understand."

Fifty-One

Office of Dr. Serian Carver, MD, Neurophysiologist

The following morning, Dr. Nelson joined Dr. Carver in his office for a preliminary review of the results while Tova and Arben waited in another room.

Dr. Carver studied the screen for a moment before his face filled with anger. "Dammit!" he snapped. He pulled up the session's documentation. "It appears the tech failed to calibrate the machine."

As Dr. Carver reviewed the log files, confirming that the machine was indeed calibrated, Dr. Nelson politely said, "Forgive me, doctor, but nothing about Mr. Davis has been normal. Is it possible that his brain activity is also off the charts? Could he be some sort of savant?"

"Nonsense."

"He tested beyond three standard deviations for hearing

sensitivity in my office. And, by the way, he and Tova are waiting outside to hear the results."

"Fine. Send them in. But doctor," Dr. Carver said condescendingly, "These scans are the result of a mechanical failure, not some meaningful discovery. However, I'll humor you just to prove there's nothing useful in this kludge."

Dr. Carver returned his attention to the results on the screen. Within moments, his expression changed dramatically. He was completely absorbed by what he was seeing, flipping through image after image.

Tova and Arben quietly entered the room and took their seats, waiting for the doctor to speak. Dr. Carver pushed back from the console and said, "This is not a tumor or a cyst. It is some sort of malformation in the inner ear, one like I've never seen."

He looked at the screen again, captivated by the images. After a few minutes, he again pushed back from the console.

"Absolutely amazing," he murmured. "I once read about a man in the 1400s who had a deformed inner ear. He was caught talking to the wind, labeled as crazy, and subsequently imprisoned."

"Sounds familiar," Dr. Nelson commented, flashing an embarrassed grin at Arben.

Dr. Carver continued, "Academics theorized the deformity distorted the sound entering his ear, which influenced the formation of his initial neural commitments."

"What does that mean?" Tova asked.

"When an infant hears one language over and over, the brain forms connections between what it hears and what the brain *understands*. These connections—neural commitments—are what we recognize as language. The man with the deformed ear couldn't distinguish between sound and language, so his brain created neural commitments for every sound."

"Are you saying that his brain treated all sound as language?" Tova asked.

"That's the theory," Dr. Carver said.

"Did they fix it?" Arben asked.

"Goodness, no. It was the fifteenth century. They were happy just to see the age of thirty."

"No," Arben repeated sadly, hearing what sounded like yet another doctor telling him he couldn't be fixed.

"That was a long time ago," Dr. Carver said, responding to the disappointment in Arben's voice. "There's no telling what we could've done for that man today."

"Modern surgical techniques can correct many abnormalities," Dr. Nelson interjected.

Arben nodded, uncertain if he was hearing anything more than false hope.

Dr. Carver further dashed his dreams, saying, "With the placement of this anomaly and the intermingled connective tissue, surgery would likely be ill-advised."

"You can't fix it." Arben said.

"I'm saying surgery is probably not the answer. There are a lot of nerves involved, and surgery could make matters worse. The risk is significant. Surgery could leave you unable to understand anything."

"I don't want that," Arben muttered, his outlook dimming further.

"Arben," Dr. Carver said, his tone gentle. "This is unchartered territory for all of us."

"That's right," Dr. Nelson added. "Knowing what is there—this growth—is only the first step."

Tova took Arben's hand. "They're right, Arben. A week ago, we had no idea what was happening. Now, we know this thing has been there your entire life."

"It doesn't matter," Arben said dejectedly. "I can't be fixed."

Dr. Carver looked at Arben. "Listen, I'm not ready to give up. I have a world-class team of specialists. When they put their collective minds together, anything is possible."

Desperately, Tova asked, "Is it at least safe for him to return to performing?"

"Arben needs full-time ear protection until we have a better understanding of what this is," Dr. Carver replied.

Arben sighed. "No. Not with earplugs. It sounds bad, and I don't want to play."

Dr. Nelson chimed in. "Arben, be sensible. As it is, you're likely destroying your hearing."

"Not to mention the side effects," Dr. Carver added. "You're literally living in a cacophonous world, as we saw from the MRI. The average person hears noise, which the brain dismisses. But your brain works in overdrive, trying to sort through a constant barrage of chaos. It works infinitely harder, which I can only conclude is very taxing."

Dr. Carver paused, pulled out his phone, and sent a quick message. "I'm enlisting my best people to study these images and develop a comprehensive analysis. Perhaps we can come up with a treatment that doesn't involve a prohibitively risky surgery with unpredictable outcomes."

"How long will that take?" Tova asked. "I'd like to book a few gigs as soon as possible."

"I believe Arben should absolutely avoid loud environments unless he has adequate ear protection," Dr. Nelson remarked.

Arben slowly shook his head. "I don't want to play with earplugs."

Everyone in the room felt the sadness in his voice.

Dr. Carver turned to Arben. "With effective ear protection, I see no reason why you can't return to performing immediately, especially since you don't seem to have any hearing loss."

"He's been slowly getting worse," Tova said, "leading up to… the episode where the voices said a fire was coming."

"I heard them," Arben stated defensively, feeling excluded from the conversation.

"Yes," Dr. Carver acknowledged. "There's no doubt you hear things no one else hears."

Arben glared at the doctor, perceiving his words as a dismissal of the voices being real. He emphatically said, "I heard them because they are real. It's *not* my imagination."

Dr. Carver smiled. "That's not what I meant. The voices *are* real. I believe that one hundred percent. And they are coming from outside your mind. It's just that your brain is the only one capable of turning everyday sounds into voices. I don't believe that's something you're causing or have any control over."

Arben stared at the doctor, baffled by his words but slowly starting to unravel their meaning.

Fifty-Two

Office of Dr. Serian Carver, MD, Neurophysiologist

As Arben thought about Dr. Carver's words, a comforting realization began to emerge. *He believes me and it's not my fault*, he told himself.

"So, it's this thing in my ear? All of it?" Arben asked.

Dr. Carver nodded. "I believe so."

"So, if you took it out, I'd be fixed?"

"Theoretically, yes. But it's not that simple. You've had this thing your entire life, and it has been feeding—jumbling—the messages going to your brain. Removing it might solve some problems, but your brain has adapted to interpreting the sounds this *thing* has sent to it over the years."

Arben retreated into his own thoughts, connecting dots he had never imagined possible. A feeling of enlightenment pulsed through him as he realized his problems stemmed from a physical condition, and were not his fault. The guilt he had carried, believing he was responsible for his situation, began to lift. Instead of seeing himself as mentally damaged and inadequate, he started to view himself as an innocent victim of something far beyond his control.

"But it's not my fault?" Arben asked rhetorically, reflecting on his mother's belief that he had created his own nightmare.

"That's right," Dr, Carver said. "This is a congenital defect that has been with you since birth."

"God's not punishing me?"

Dr. Carver chuckled. "Of course not. This isn't something you caused or have any control over."

Tova was pleased by the doctor's words. She had been counseling Arben in her own way, trying to teach him the truth about the Bible and how his mother had filled his head with falsehoods and distortions. It had been a slow and delicate task because Tova didn't want to speak ill of the dead or disparage the mother Arben loved.

Dr. Carver continued, "And, if my hypothesis is correct, your neural mapping is complete chaos. I need time to consider the implications. But until we know for sure, ear protection is mandatory if you choose to perform. We will also biopsy the growths."

Deep inside, Arben was yearning to perform, but earplugs had always been a deal breaker. However, having been away from performing for a few weeks and learning that his struggles weren't of his own making, he began to rethink his position. He hated earplugs and was still opposed to wearing them during a performance, but in that moment of vindication, he wasn't ruling anything out.

"I don't want to play with earplugs…" Arben started, his thoughts spilling out. "But maybe."

Dr. Nelson interjected, "Doctor, according to Dr. Andrews, the psyche doctor at Tarrant County MHSC, Arben could function while wearing noise-cancelling headphones. He concluded it was the hum of a soda machine and/or the transformers that ran the security system that caused the crippling effect. And, my initial hearing tests showed an unusual sensitivity to lower frequencies."

Dr. Carver said, "The frequency sweep confirms there is a correlation between his discomfort and low frequencies."

"Dr. Andrews and I both observed in the first MRI that the Vent changes."

"The Vent?" Dr. Carver questioned.

"The growth looks like an air vent. You called them striations. When we ran the images as a sequence, we observed changes in the anomaly."

Dr. Carver furrowed his brow and said, "Let's look at the frequency sweep." He brought up the corresponding images on the screen, showing the moment Arben ripped off the headphones.

"My God!" Dr. Carver exclaimed. "His cerebrum exploded with activity. It appears to have been quite unpleasant."

"Something happens when the frequency drops below 65 hertz," Dr. Nelson remarked.

Dr. Carver ran the series of images several times, clearly intrigued by what he was seeing. "This is quite astonishing. That much distortion would impact all the auditory nerves." He turned away from the screen, shaking his head in amazement. "This is an extraordinary discovery."

He glanced at his watch and reluctantly rose from the desk. "I have several obligations to attend to, but I'll immediately put my team on this." Turning to Arben, he extended his hand and said, "Arben. I want to see you in my office in six weeks—possibly sooner if we have a breakthrough. Someone from my office will call you."

Fifty-Three

Tova's Car, Ft. Worth, Texas

Arben was quiet on the drive home from the meeting with Dr. Carver, trying to sort through everything the doctors had discovered.

"It's hard to believe all this," Tova said, attempting to engage Arben.

"It's not my fault," he said aloud, still reveling in his realization.

"What isn't?"

"Everything. Mom said I was evil. God was punishing me. She said I had bad karma. Dad said I didn't listen. The voices are not my imagination." His tone was confident and celebratory, but tinged with remorse.

Cautiously, Tova said, "Arben, I know you loved your mother and I want you to hold on to that feeling."

Arben gave her a puzzled look, aware that Arlene didn't like

Tova and his love for his mother was complicated.

"But now that you *know* you're not evil and God *isn't* punishing you like your mother said, I want you to read the Bible for yourself and pray." She paused, noticing his confusion. "We've talked a little about what the Bible *actually* says and how it differs from what your mom said."

"Mom talked a lot about God."

"Yes, well… I know you're beginning to understand that not everything she taught you is correct. Everyone eventually learns that their parents never had all the answers, but the Bible does. I've told you this before, and I'll probably say it again, but I believe each person should get to know God on their own, not through the messages they hear from their parents, friends, or even their minister. If you read the Bible on your own and pray, I think you'll find out for yourself what it all means. Of course, you and I and others should talk about it, but in the end, it's really between you and God."

He nodded. "I know. Mom said stuff that I don't believe anymore, but there's a lot I don't know."

Tova smiled. "That's good. Welcome to the club. Realizing that you don't have all the answers is a major step forward. No one does. The best place to find answers is in the Bible."

"Okay, but I don't like to read."

She laughed. "A lot of people are like that. But I tell you what, you and I can make it a point to read more while we're on the road. That way we can also talk about what it means. I don't have all the answers either, but I don't mind discussing it."

He smiled. "Okay."

"The more you learn about God and Christ, the more you'll discover about what a wonderful person you are and how truly blessed you are."

Arben nodded, though his expression turned sad. "But Mom and Dad won't ever know."

"No, they won't, and that's a shame. But you should look forward rather than backward. Never forget the past, but don't let it hold you there."

After a long silence, Arben let his thoughts spill out. "They still can't fix me. I'll always be like this."

"Maybe so. But that's something you pray about. I believe God will help guide you through this hearing thing." She paused, giving him space to absorb her words. "No matter what the doctors do, you're still an amazing pianist with a bright future. You're not crazy, and you're not causing bad things to happen to other people. God's not punishing you. You're a gifted young man with your whole life ahead of you."

Her words helped, but Arben still felt weighed down by depression. The idea that he might never perform again without earplugs was a dark cloud that wouldn't go away.

"I wanted to be normal," Arben confessed. Tova opened her mouth to respond, but he cut her off. "I know. Normal people can't play like I do."

"I wish I had an answer for that, Arben. But I don't. And the road forward may still be difficult. There's a phrase you'll hear now and then: we all have our crosses to bear." He shook his head, confused. "It means none of us are perfect and we all have problems—like your hearing—that weigh us down." Arben nodded, letting the lesson sink in. "Everyone has problems, but they aren't punishment from God," she added. "It's God who will help you carry the burden."

Fifty-Four

Residence of Tova and David Rawlins

When Arben and Tova arrived home from Dr. Carver's office, David was there waiting. Tova had texted him some details of their meeting, and he was eager to hear the rest.

"What a day, huh?" David remarked, shaking Arben's hand and giving Tova a quick kiss. Their lukewarm reception surprised him. "Am I missing something? They figured it out, didn't they?"

"I'm sorry honey," Tova said. "They left us with more unanswered questions."

"Like what?"

Arben unexpectedly chimed in, his irritation evident. "They want me to wear earplugs. I can't play with earplugs. It sounds bad, and it feels bad." He scowled, on the verge of launching into a rant.

But then, he paused and released a heavy sigh. "It's all I have," he said defeatedly. "And it's going away."

"No, it's not," Tova immediately responded.

"Yes, it is!" Arben snapped, tears forming in his eyes. "I don't want to play if I have to wear earplugs."

David put a hand on Arben's shoulder and walked him toward the den. "Arben, we're on your side. Let's talk this through."

Tova frequently joked that she had married a diplomat. She was grateful that her husband was taking the lead, knowing Arben had grown up with very little male influence in his life.

David pointed Arben to a comfortable chair and asked, "You want some tea, a soda, water?"

Arben nodded and quietly said, "Water."

Tova retrieved a bottle for him, along with a glass of wine for herself.

"Arben," Tova said, handing him the water. "They didn't say you *have* to wear earplugs."

"Yes, they did," he fired back, frustrated by the finality of the doctor's conclusions. "They said I would damage my hearing."

"You *might* damage your hearing," Tova corrected. "But remember, you've been performing live for almost a year now, and they said your hearing is still exceptional."

"Sounds like they're wrong about the damage thing," David commented. "But let's talk about what they actually said."

Tova filled David in on all the details.

"That's amazing, Arben," David remarked.

"Amazing that I have a tumor and have to quit playing?" Arben sarcastically stated.

"No. It's amazing that you've had this condition your entire life and yet here you are, a world-class pianist, thrilling audiences and making it into one of the most prestigious competitions in the world."

"I didn't make it past the audition."

"One in a thousand make it *to* the audition, and none of them had to overcome what you've done so far," David said, pausing and speaking more oratorically. "You see, it's all about perspective. Most people would kill to get there."

"Most would kill to have one tenth of your talent," Tova added. "Not to mention your creativity." She turned to David. "I told him he was blessed, and the more he seeks out the Holy Spirit, the more he'll see God working in his life."

David nodded. "Exactly. Arben, what you're seeing as failure is actually success against very long odds. That makes you a one-in-a-million. And if you're that special, I don't believe you're finished, no matter what the doctors say. Tova's right. You *have* been blessed, but I understand that it's hard to see when you've spent your entire life struggling with this burden. Turn it over to God."

Arben absorbed David's words and wanted to feel optimistic, but all he could imagine was playing while wearing earplugs. "Why play if it doesn't sound good?"

"Do your ears hurt when you play?" David asked.

"A little when they clap, if there's a lot of people."

"But not when you're actually playing?"

Arben shook his head.

"That's kind of a high-class problem," David said with a chuckle. "You see, you can play all you want without ear protection, as long as you cover your ears or put the plugs in when they applaud."

"It also gets loud when I don't know it's coming," Arben said.

"That's the problem," Tova said. "It seems this thing in his ears amplifies the sound without warning."

"Okay," David said optimistically. "But that's what Dr. Carver is going to figure out. And when he does, they'll find a way for you to play again."

Arben shook his head in defeat. "No. They won't operate. That's how they fix it. I might have cancer."

David glanced at Tova for verification. She gave a sad nod as Arben rose and started for his room. "I should go home," he resignedly said.

"Home?" Tova asked. "We see this as your home. At least for now."

"I should go home. To my house."

Tova hated to reveal what she'd learned from Ms. Railey. "Arben, your mom's house was a rental."

"Okay," he said, not recognizing the implications.

"When she passed, the landlord boxed up all her belongings and moved them to a storage facility. You can still get them, but you can't return to the house."

"I can't go home, ever?"

"I'm afraid not. Ms. Railey said you're always welcome at her house, but David and I want you to stay here, especially until we see what Dr. Carver does."

I can't go home, echoed in Arben's mind. A part of him felt completely alone and lost. "Okay," he murmured with a heavy sigh as he wandered from the den to his bedroom.

In the dark, he lay on the bed, consumed with self-pity. *I can't play anymore. They can't fix me. I can't go home. I don't have a home. I have cancer. I could die.* The ceiling above seemed to mirror his life: dark, quiet, and lonely. *God, I need help... but I can't be fixed...* He inhaled deeply and released a huge sigh.

With Arben out of the room, Tova pulled out her list of contacts and said, "He just needs to get in front of a crowd."

"You think it's safe?" David asked.

"You saw him. His life is over if he can't play. Safe or not, I won't risk him giving up to the point he..." She remembered the ER doctor suggesting that Arben's lake jump might have been a suicide attempt. "I will *not* let him give up."

Fifty-Five

On the road

After Dr. Carver cleared Arben to perform, Tova booked a handful of dates. However, she was deeply concerned about the possibility of him having another episode and purchased a variety of earplugs as a precaution.

Driving to the first performance, Tova pulled out a pair and said, "I got several types to see if any of them work better than what you've had in the past."

"No. David said I can play without them," Arben replied.

"He's not a doctor, and I don't want you affected by sudden loud noise or voices distracting you."

"I can play when the voices talk."

"But I've seen how the loud noise affects you—you can't play when it hits."

Arben wanted to dig his heels in but knew she was right.

He reluctantly put the earplugs in but quickly removed them, muttering, "I feel pressure in my head."

"Try some of the other ones."

He went through several pairs, but each had the same result. Frustrated, Arben declared, "I can't play with them."

Tova found herself in a tough spot. She didn't want to risk an unexpected sound throwing him off, yet forcing the issue might lead to him refusing to perform altogether.

Tova, in her most convincing voice, said, "Arben, we'll be seeing the doctor in a few weeks. Maybe they'll have good news, maybe they won't. But until then, can you please follow their advice and wear the earplugs?"

Arben drew in a deep breath, ready to protest, but Tova raised a hand to stop him. "Hear me out. Yes, it'll sound bad and yes, you'll feel pressure in your ears. And *maybe* it won't be fun, but the audience will still love you, they'll still applaud, and they'll want to hear more. Only you and I will know what you're going through."

She leaned closer, her tone softening, but firm. "Think of how it feels to listen to a great performer like yourself? Please, Arben. Just try. It's only for a few gigs, and I know you can do it. Trust that Dr. Carver will have good news. But even if he doesn't, you're still among the most talented pianists in the country. You *must* keep playing even if it means wearing ear protection. Do it for me. Do it for yourself. You've worked your whole life getting here. Do it for the people who love hearing you play. God gave you this great gift for a reason. You have to share it with the world."

Arben couldn't refuse.

During the first performance, Arben fiddled with the earplugs and found it difficult to enjoy playing. However, he managed to complete the set without any major setbacks. Soon enough, they were on their way to the next performance.

At two private parties that followed, Arben persistently complained to Tova about the earplugs. While performing, he often removed them despite her objections.

Each night brought more guests to Tova, eager to book Arben for future events. Though uneasy, she continued adding dates to his schedule, knowing the earplugs were becoming a dealbreaker.

After one show, as soon as they got in the car, Arben yanked the earplugs out and declared, "I don't want to do this anymore."

"But you've been doing better," Tova replied.

"Only when I pull these out," he countered.

She could feel the frustration and decided to tread carefully. "Well," she said, thinking about how well he'd been doing without the earplugs. "Are you feeling pain when the applause starts?"

"Some," he admitted. "But it's not bad."

"And the voices? Are you hearing any? Are they distracting?"

"I always hear them. But they sound normal."

"Other than the earplugs, are you enjoying playing?"

A small smile broke through his frustration as he nodded.

She considered the options before saying, "Let's try the next gig without them, but keep them in your pocket or on the piano. And promise me you'll put them in the moment you feel pain."

"Okay."

Though Tova knew this compromise was risky, she decided to let him proceed on his terms for now. At their next gig, Arben occasionally twisted and turned but hid his discomfort well.

Fifty-Six

Bent Tree Country Club, North Dallas, Texas

On the morning of Arben's final show of the week, Dr. Carver's office unexpectedly called on a Sunday to schedule a meeting for Monday morning.

The event was a brunch at a small, open-air pavilion at the Bent Tree Country Club, nestled in a Dallas suburb. With the guests eagerly awaiting his performance, Arben stood with Tova near the piano. Notably, he wasn't wearing earplugs.

The party organizer approached with a polite smile and said, "They are ready for you, Mr. Davis."

As Tova gave Arben a quick good-luck hug, the compressor on a portable ice maker kicked on, emitting a low hum. At first, the sound merely startled Arben, but within moments, it became an overwhelming roar in his head. He clutched Tova's shoulders, his expression twisted in pain.

All at once, the surrounding sounds—the distant hum of a city bus, the rumble of the crowd, and the faint whir of a nearby freeway—collided into a deafening cacophony. Arben let go of Tova and grabbed his ears. "Oh God, it hurts!" he cried out.

Reacting swiftly, Tova turned him away from the gathering crowd and pointed him toward a nearby restroom. "Walk to the restroom," she instructed firmly, keeping her composure as she hurried them away from the stage.

Before following him fully, Tova briefly faced the party organizer, raising a finger as if to silently communicate, 'One moment, please.'

Inside the bathroom, Arben paced frantically, clutching his ears. Both he and Tova looked panicked. Tova wasted no time, pulling out a spare set of earplugs. "Here. Put these in."

He shook his head in frustration.

"Arben," she said firmly, "we're seeing Dr. Carver tomorrow morning. Please, put them in so you can finish the performance."

"Why does this keep happening!" Arben cried out, anger and pain surging through him. He grunted a final blast of irritation then reluctantly inserted the earplugs. On the verge of tears, he said, "This is the last time."

Tova's heart sank. She felt as though all the progress Arben had made was lost in an instant. Placing a comforting hand on his arm, she locked eye with him. "Arben, listen to me. You've been through this before. Focus. Go out there and give them a great performance. Tomorrow, we'll figure this out together."

Arben wiped away a single tear as it slid down his cheek.

"You can do this," she reassured him.

He nodded, and she escorted him back to the piano. Before he sat down, she gave him a quick wink and an encouraging smile.

Despite the muffled sound of the piano and the pressure in his head, Arben delivered two impressive forty-five-minute sets. The crowd was mesmerized, and their roaring standing ovation at the end filled the pavilion. Arben bowed deeply, a faint but bittersweet smile on his face.

After the performance, Arben stood beside the piano as guests streamed past, shaking his hand and showering him with compliments. Frustrated by the earplugs and barely able to hear their words, he gave in to a moment of exasperation, pulling the earplugs out and tossing them to the ground. He turned his head from side to side, testing for discomfort. Sensing no immediate issue, he smiled and resumed greeting the remaining guests.

As the crowd thinned and Arben happily interacted with a few lingering fans, a low, powerful hum from an industrial generator several blocks away at the Addison Airfield began. While others remained oblivious, the thunderous explosion reverberated inside Arben's head.

With pain consuming his ears, Arben twisted and turned violently until the pain built to an unbearable peak. "Ow!" he cried, clutching his ears.

Tova was next to him and noticed the discarded earplugs on the ground. She acted quickly, pulling him aside and retrieving her final spare pair. "Put these in. Now," she quietly ordered.

He complied while she turned to the fans with an apologetic smile. "Thank you all. I'm sorry, but we have to run."

She ushered Arben to the car, backing away quickly to avoid

further questions.

During the drive home, Arben's frustration boiled over. "That's it," he declared. "I quit. I hate earplugs. I hate playing with them. I hate loud noises and I just want it to end. I quit."

His voice trembled with raw emotion, and though his frustration replaced tears, it was clear just how close he was to breaking.

Tova sat silently for a moment, absorbing his pain before she finally spoke. "I know," she said gently. "But thank you for putting in the earplugs and finishing the performance with dignity."

"No more!" he snapped.

"There's got to be a solution," she said, sounding desperate. Turning to him, she added, "You can't quit."

With tears glistening in his eyes, Arben stared at her for a long moment. Finally, he slowly closed his eyes and nodded.

Fifty-Seven

Office of Dr. Serian Carver, MD, Neurophysiologist

Dr. Carver and his team gathered in the state-of-the-art conference room, featuring a large table in the center and multiple computer screens mounted on the walls and suspended from the ceiling. Seated at the table were members of Dr. Carver's team, along with Drs. Nelson and Andrews. Dr. Carver stood at one end of the table as Arben and Tova entered.

"There they are," Dr. Carver announced. "Everyone, please welcome Arben and Tova." He gestured toward two chairs. "Please, have a seat."

Dr. Carver then introduced the team, spreading his arms wide. "These brilliant individuals are part of my research and development team. They represent some of the brightest minds in the country. They have been working tirelessly, and we think you're going to like what you *hear*."

His remarks drew a chuckle from the team. "So, without further ado..." He pressed a button on the remote control, displaying an image on a large screen. "What you're seeing here is now officially known as Arben's Vent. It's a combination of skin, cartilage, and ganglion or nerve tissue that formed proximal to the tympanic membrane or eardrum. It has been there since birth and is a permanent part of Arben's neural network."

He then switched to a new image of the anomaly. "Similar to the air conditioning vents you see in most houses, Arben's Vent has fins or vents running laterally, hence the name. Because of the fins and the manner in which they react to sound, Arben's hearing and the development of his neural network have been profoundly impacted. Although our research is still ongoing, we've confirmed that Arben's Vent causes him to hear sound in ways that are entirely unique to him. Consequently, his brain has learned to interpret and understand sounds in ways that science has never seen before. But I'm getting ahead of myself. Allow me to say that this small anomaly will have a significant impact on the study of neurology." He once again spread his arms. "These talented individuals have mapped and modeled the Vent and have actually constructed a working replica. Using 3-D printing technology, we created a functional model, which we took to a specialized audio lab where they were able to simulate what Arben hears."

Arben hung on every word.

Dr. Carver started a video showing a quiet room with a table at its center. On the table, a microphone was positioned over a dish. A buzzing sound began as Dr. Carver paused the video.

"Okay," he said. "Everyone heard the buzzing sound produced

by the noise generator. Next, we simulated Arben's eardrum by placing a membrane next to the 3-D model of the Vent. We fed the same buzzing sounds into the Vent and recorded what the membrane heard."

He clicked a button, and another video began. Tova was intrigued as everyone heard a mumbling sound—like distant conversation—emanating from the video. Arben remained expressionless.

Dr. Carver paused the video. "We were absolutely astonished to learn how the Vent alters everything Arben hears. We replaced the noise generator with a man and woman. The man says, 'good afternoon,' and the woman replies, 'nice weather we're having.'"

He rolled a video that showed exactly what he had described. "Now, this is what Arben hears." He pressed the button, and the images were the same—the man and woman speaking—but everyone in the room, except Arben, heard a whooshing and clicking sound. It sounded nothing like voices.

"How is that possible?" Tova asked. "He understands every word he hears." She turned to Arben. "What did you hear?"

Arben shrugged and said, "Good afternoon. Nice weather."

"Both times?" Tova asked. Arben nodded. "Do you hear everything I say?" she asked.

Arben nodded. "I *hear* everything. Sometimes it doesn't sound right."

"What do you mean, it doesn't sound right?" Tova pressed.

"Like sound, noise," he answered with another shrug. "Not really words."

"Then how do you know what I'm saying, or what anyone's

saying?"

Arben pondered for a moment. "I don't know. I hear your voice and words sometimes. Sometimes sounds. I don't know how I understand. How do you understand what I'm saying?"

Dr. Carver intervened. "He understands some of what he hears, but he poses a key question. Learning to understand language is a complex process, but for Arben, the process was further complicated. We really unlocked this part of the puzzle with the help of someone from Arben's past."

Arben perked up when a researcher—a young woman wearing a lab coat—stood and steadied herself using the table. His eyes lit up. "Olivia," he said softly.

Fifty-Eight

Office of Dr. Serian Carver, MD, Neurophysiologist

Hello Arben," Olivia said with an ear-to-ear grin.

"Olivia is one of my undergrads interning as a researcher," Dr. Carver explained. "When she saw Arben's name, she immediately knew who he was." He turned to Olivia and yielded the floor to her.

"Arben, it's great to see you. I've thought about you a lot. You're one of the reasons I went into science. When we were kids, nature didn't always talk to you. Sometimes you said you heard the birds singing and other times they talked. But one constant was that you always heard distant mumbling. I told Dr. Carver about the persistent mumbling, and he confirmed his original hypothesis that your brain was interpreting *all* sounds, except music, as language. No one had ever seen that before."

"Including me," Dr. Carver interjected.

Olivia continued, "Once we realized you weren't perceiving sounds as they actually are, but what you believed to be language, or what your brain interpreted as language, Dr. Carver suggested we analyze your MRI results like those of a person with diminished hearing or someone who doesn't hear words clearly. When the brain doesn't receive enough information to form a conclusion or understand well enough to make a decision, it tries to fill in the missing information. It's similar to when you're reading a book and come across a word you've never seen or heard. You can understand the meaning simply by the context. If a sentence describes a painful experience but uses an unfamiliar word for discomfort, your brain still gets the gist of the sentence. So, when you, Arben, hear the mumbling, we believe your brain is treating those sounds as if it's hearing words it doesn't recognize, and it tries to fill in the missing information."

"And that causes him pain?" Tova asked.

"Oh no," Olivia replied. "It simply explains how Arben's learning developed. I'll let the doctor explain the rest." She awkwardly lowered herself back into her chair.

"We'll come back to that," Dr. Carver said, directing everyone's attention to the screen where he clicked on an enlarged rendering of Arben's Vent. He pointed to the rows of thin, elastic vents running the length of the growth. "It's not uncommon for a structure like this to resonate or vibrate when acted upon, like when wind from your breath passes between the vocal cords. The wind causes the cords to vibrate—higher if they are tightened and more slowly if they are long and relaxed. What's unusual about Arben's Vent is how it responds to low frequencies but not high ones. We don't completely understand why, but when we applied a frequency sweep through the Vent, the results were quite remarkable. When certain low frequencies strike the Vent, the fins change in ways that cause extraordinary amplification."

Arben raised his hand, stopping Dr. Carver.

"Yes Arben?"

"I don't feel anything different. I just hear a noise getting louder. A lot louder."

"Do you notice sounds getting louder when you play the lowest notes on the piano?" Dr. Carver asked.

Arben immediately nodded. "Low F, G, and A. I substitute higher ones or different notes. That's why I change the music."

"Interesting," Dr. Carver remarked. "So, playing those low notes has bothered you for a long time?"

Arben nodded. "I play D for F and E for G, sometimes softer, or I change the chord so it still sounds good but doesn't bother me."

The room buzzed with amazement at Arben's ability to compensate and adapt.

Dr. Carver raised his hands to quiet the murmuring as Arben asked, "What does it look like? The Vent thing, when I hit F?"

"I can show you," Dr. Carver said, lighting up Arben's face. He started a video to illustrate what he was describing.

"It is much like when waves collide in a pool of water. If you drop a rock into a calm pond, the waves ripple across the water, progressively slowing down until they completely dissipate, or hit the other side. When they hit the other side, the ripples bounce off the shore and reverse course, colliding with the original waves. Many of the ripples or waves are destroyed in the collision.

However, if you drop two rocks in a pond—one right after the other—the faster ripples generated by the second rock will catch the slowing ripples from the first rock and amplify them. This is analogous to what is happening, Arben. The Vents in your ears are always vibrating, but when they're struck with just the right frequency, it's like when the ripples of two waves combine into one larger ripple. The resulting sounds is an amplified version of the combined waves. This is known as constructive interference. The sound is louder because the waves or ripples are being added together into progressively larger, louder sounds.

We theorize that when the Vent is acted upon by a combination of low frequencies and volume, constructive interference is created. This combination of low frequencies at a certain volume—like those created by the vending machine—sends the Vents into overdrive, thus producing the extreme volume, and perhaps part of what's producing what you perceive as voices. Although, the voices may also be part of your neurology."

Dr. Carver turned and addressed the entire room. "His brain has been trying to understand what it hears for his entire life. Many of the thousands of signals his ears send to his brain every day may have been misinterpreted, such as the sound of trees blowing being interpreted as voices."

"I'm confused," Tova said. "You're telling me that the hum from the vending machine speaks a language he understands?"

"The low hum from the soda machine produces a frequency that *triggers* the Vent, which causes the loud volume," Dr. Carver corrected. "It differs from the language his brain processes from most sounds. Additionally, Arben's brain is overly taxed trying to process infinitely more sounds than a typical brain because it perceives every sound as language with inherent meaning. And, as Olivia explained, it is all that incomplete information his brain is trying to make sense of."

"Unbelievable," Tova said. "He's told me about hearing voices since early childhood, but why hasn't the loudness always been a problem?"

Arben responded, "Sometimes it was loud in my backyard when I was young, and when Dad played his guitar. When Dad's band practiced, the drums and bass hurt."

"I suspect there were many times when that happened," Dr. Carver said.

"But no one did anything," Arben said sadly, reflecting on all the times he'd complained to teachers, parents, doctors, and other adults. Back then, Arben believed no one cared enough to answer his calls for help.

"This is new to everyone," Dr. Carver said. "I wish I had all the answers. I do agree that someone should have taken you seriously a long time ago, but I don't know that anyone could have figured this out. It took some very sophisticated equipment and a team of specialists to get this far. I would probably be a little disillusioned myself if I had lived nineteen years struggling with this. But try not to fixate on the past."

Arben gave a slightly derisive snort but nodded.

Fifty-Nine

Office of Dr. Serian Carver, MD, Neurophysiologist

Standing at the head of the table in the conference room, Dr. Carver paused for a sip of water before resuming his explanation to Arben. "The loudness you experienced probably wasn't as problematic when you were young because as you grew physically, the Vent also grew. When it was small, it probably didn't move as freely. Imagine holding a very short string in front of a fan. It will vibrate, but in a tight range. Contrast that with a long string that vibrates across a much wider range. You probably started having greater problems once you hit a growth spurt. At that point, the Vent grew large enough to produce a standing wave or maintain a resonance long enough to amplify the sound and thus produce pain. Before that, the Vent simply sent unusual sounds to your brain, which your brain tried to make sense of."

"Like the wishing trees?" Arben asked.

"Yes," Dr. Carver said. "The wishing trees. For those of you who don't know what that means…" He paused and turned to Arben. "I'll let Mr. Davis explain it."

Arben smiled, finally able to talk about something that had always drawn ridicule. "I always heard the trees in the backyard telling me to wish." He paused, glancing at Dr. Carver, an embarrassed smile spreading across his face. "They weren't really telling me that, were they?" He felt foolish for asking but was relieved to learn the truth.

Dr. Carver smiled, finding Arben's revelation endearing. "To anyone else, I would say no, they weren't. But to you, they were. It's astonishing how well you've adjusted. Anyone else in your situation would likely never have learned to talk and would've been institutionalized at a young age. I suspect you have an extraordinarily high IQ, but that's neither here nor there."

Arben's mind brimmed with new understanding as he processed the doctor's findings. "So, I *was* hearing voices, and they *were* telling me to wish," Arben asked rhetorically. "But only because this vent thing was making me hear differently than everyone else."

A deep sense of vindication swept over him. *I knew they were real,* he thought. Sitting silently, he smiled as thoughts of validation ran through his mind, recalling all the times he was told things like, "it's your imagination" or the one he heard most often, "I don't hear anything." He remembered the incredulous looks he got from doctors, teachers, and even his mother, who all thought he was crazy. *I kinda thought I was crazy, too,* he admitted to himself, releasing an internal chuckle. Now, he found it amusing to revisit those frustrating moments when he *knew* he wasn't crazy.

"So how do we deal with this?" Tova asked, trying to grasp the complexity of the situation. "I'm afraid to book anything if some unknown or far-off sound could freak him out, or worse, damage his hearing."

Dr. Nelson chimed in, "I believe ear protection is mandatory."

"No!" Arben stated sharply. "I'm not playing with earplugs."

Dr. Andrews added, "We had success using noise-cancelling headphones, but I don't see how that would work for a piano concert."

"He gets frustrated and usually pulls the earplugs out," Tova said.

Arben nodded. "I feel pressure. I *can* play, but I don't like it. Can't you take this thing… this vent thing out?" he pleaded.

"I'd like nothing better," Dr. Carver said, "But you already know the answer. It's just too risky."

Arben sighed, his tone soaked with frustration and despair. "I'm stuck with it."

Sixty

Office of Dr. Serian Carver, MD, Neurophysiologist

While Arben was on a rollercoaster of emotions—up when Dr. Carver explained his malady, down when he heard that it couldn't be removed—he expressed his despair, saying, "I'm going to be like this forever."

Dr. Carver gave Arben a sly smile and picked up a small box from the table. "Not necessarily," he said, setting the box in front of Arben. "Open it."

Arben opened the box and saw a pair of earplugs. He gritted his teeth and was about to scream but held back. Instead, he sharply barked, "I hate these!" He quickly slammed the box shut and shoved it away.

Dr. Carver snickered. "Those are special earplugs, Arben. I think you'll like them. They're prototypes, so we still have some adjustments to make—working out the fitting and fine-tuning the design. Please, put them in."

"Why?" Arben asked angrily. "I won't play if I have to wear them."

Tova slid the box over and opened it. She took out one earplug and examined it. "These are different, Arben. Try one. What do you have to lose? If they really are different, maybe you can play while wearing them. You don't *really* want to quit playing, do you?"

Arben reluctantly put one plug in his ear and immediately wrinkled his brow, then twisted and turned his head. Unlike every earplug he'd worn before, these didn't make his head feel like it was full of pressure. He put the second one in, turned his head, and said, "A-flat."

Tova and Olivia laughed.

"I remember this," Olivia said. "He telling us the pitch of something."

Arben looked up and pointed. "The lights."

Everyone in the room carefully listened to the faint buzz coming from the fluorescent lights. Most laughed, astonished, and entertained.

"What else do you hear?" Dr. Carver asked.

"Everything," Arben said. "These are broken."

The doctor and his team laughed as Arben removed the earplugs.

"Those are special earplugs that filter out certain frequencies," Dr. Carver said. "Other than the specific low frequencies that activate the Vent, you'll hear everything. You could and perhaps should wear them all the time. While you will still hear some anomalies like the voices, those earplugs will prevent the sounds from becoming excessively loud."

Dr. Carver set a metal box with a big red button in front of Arben. "We're going to do a little experiment. Before you put the earplugs in, we're going to pipe sound into the room. It will start with a soft, high-pitched sound. The pitch will slowly descend until it's inaudible, just like the frequency sweep we did with the MRI."

Arben's eyes widened at the painful memory.

Dr. Carver chuckled. "Don't worry. If the sound becomes too loud or you hear something unusual or uncomfortable, hit that red button. That will stop the sound immediately. You have complete control."

Arben was suspicious, remembering the MRI session when the glissando caused a painful rumble that made him rip the headset off. He also recalled the day Dr. Andrews made him walk into the hall where the loudness blindsided him. He studied Dr. Carver for a moment before reluctantly nodding and putting both his hands over the button, ready to press it.

The test began. A high-pitched sound started and gradually descended. Arben remained ready to hit the button at any moment. The sound continued falling, down to a hum, then a rumble.

Suddenly, Arben flinched and said, "Uh oh." He hit the button, immediately muting the sound, and covered his ears.

"What just happened?" Tova asked.

"When certain frequencies strike Arben's ears, they activate the Vent, causing a type of harmonic. In simple terms, it supercharges the incoming sounds and delivers a blast to his inner ear."

"But wouldn't his keyboard playing do that?" Tova asked.

Dr. Carver smiled. "He just told us he avoids low F, G, and

A."

Arben confirmed the doctor's statement with a serious nod.

"We saw this clearly in the MRI when Dr. Nelson performed a frequency sweep. Once the Vent is activated, it also magnifies nearby frequencies, like the combined pond ripples, which creates the intense volume." He turned to Arben. "That blast of sound must be painful."

Arben gave a firm nod.

Dr. Carver grinned and said, "Well, those days are gone. Put the earplugs in."

Arben gave him a confused look. "But I can hear everything."

"Everything except for a narrow range of low frequencies," Dr. Carver reiterated. "Fortunately, the Vent only magnifies sound when it is activated, and it is only activated by certain frequencies. These earplugs block those. Now, please put the earplugs in. You'll see. We will perform the same test."

Arben inserted the earplugs and placed his hands over the button, doubting the earplugs would work.

Sixty-One

Office of Dr. Serian Carver, MD, Neurophysiologist

The experiment began for the second time as high-pitched sound filled the room, silencing everyone. As the pitch descended, Arben got ready to push the button. The hum transformed into a rumble, with all eyes fixed on Arben. Despite his concerned expression, he never pressed the button. They repeated the procedure several times, with and without the earplugs. The results never varied; he never pressed the button while wearing the earplugs.

Tova looked at Arben and asked, "Is the sound muffled?"

Arben fiddled with the earplugs, shaking his head in confusion. "It sounds normal."

Tova turned to Dr. Carver, her eyes filling with tears of joy. "You can't imagine what this means," she said, overwhelmed with emotion.

Arben, still bewildered, kept the earplugs in as he watched Tova. Suddenly, a big smile spread across his face. “Yes!” he shouted, drawing smiles and laughter from everyone. “Sorry,” he said, but his excitement was unstoppable. “Finally! I can do what I want. I can play! No more fear of loud applause, no noises exploding in my ears, and no more voices from nowhere.”

“You’ll likely still hear voices,” Dr. Carver cautioned. “But they won’t get loud.”

“Oh my God!” Arben proclaimed. He looked up and said, “Thank you God,” prompting an “amen” from Tova.

Arben had never felt such elation. He jumped up and shouted, “Thank you!” He stepped toward Dr. Carver to shake his hand but couldn’t help but throw his arms around the doctor for the most emotional hug he’d ever given.

“You are more than welcome,” Dr. Carver said, a little choked up, as was everyone in the room. “We will need to fine-tune the earplugs. And you’ll need additional therapy to help you understand how your brain interprets sound and language, but we can talk about all that later.”

The doctor paused, staring at Arben, momentarily amazed. “Young man, your neural profile is far beyond extraordinary. I wish I could study it every day.”

“No,” Arben immediately said with a smile. “We are going on the road.” He turned to Tova and said, “Aren’t we?”

She couldn’t hold back the tears. “Absolutely,” she said, wrapping him into a tight hug.

“You saved me,” Arben said as they separated, making no attempt to stop the tears of joy.

"*He* saved you," she replied, reaching out as Dr. Andrews approached to congratulate Arben.

Arben nodded at Tova. "Yes. Both. Everyone." He turned around to acknowledge everyone in the room. He bowed like he had just given a performance, then eked out a choked-up, "Thank you, everyone."

The meeting adjourned as the entire group gathered around Arben, patting him on the back and congratulating one another.

Later, as Arben and the team worked on fitting the earplugs and making notes on how to improve them, Tova spoke with Dr. Andrews.

"Listen, I'm throwing a party to kick off the tour that I haven't booked yet. I'll e-mail you the details. Don't disappoint me," she added playfully.

"I wouldn't miss it."

Sixty-Two

Dallas Country Club, Dallas, Texas

Tova pulled a few strings and reserved the exclusive Dallas Country Club to kick off Arben's big comeback. At one end of the elegant room stood a grand piano. Guests included familiar faces from past events, close friends of Tova and David, and some of North Texas's most influential figures. Once word got out about Arben's return, the party became the hottest ticket in town.

Tova and Arben stood near the stage, greeting guests. When the time came, Arben sat behind the piano and performed a one hour set with a look of sheer joy that never left his face. To Arben, the piano never sounded better.

Before the final set, Tova introduced Drs. Carver, Andrews, and Nelson, along with the research and development team, to the audience. "Without these people, this night wouldn't have happened," she said through tears of joy.

Arben walked over to the doctors and the team to thank them but choked up and simply bowed to them before starting to clap. The crowd cheered. The team and the doctors politely bowed, then extended their hands toward Arben and began clapping for him.

Ms. Railey stepped out of the crowd, and Arben's face lit up even brighter as tears filled his eyes. They shared a warm hug.

"I've never heard you play better," Ms. Railey said. "It was magnificent."

"Thanks to you," he said, humbly.

She chuckled. "You've thanked me enough. This day was meant to be. I told you God was on your side."

He nodded and leaned close. "I gave Him my life."

Ms. Railey leaned back with a delighted smile. "God bless you Arben."

"He did."

She smiled and said, "Yes, He did. But listen, let's talk later. This is your night."

Before starting the final set, Tova called for everyone's attention. "Arben has something special he'd like to share."

All eyes turned to Arben standing next to the piano. He was shy when it came to public speaking, so he fumbled a bit with his words.

"Many years ago, I needed a friend. And I found one. Actually, I had two, then three, and now a lot. My friend Olivia wrote me a letter."

He turned a momentary gaze at Olivia. Her eyes opened wide with anticipation of what was to come. Arben pulled out the letter Olivia had written him over ten years earlier. "I always have it with me," he said, smiling proudly at Olivia.

He turned his attention to Ms. Railey. "You have always been my friend, and you taught me how to play the piano." Then he looked at Tova. "And you are my friend. You saved me."

Arben struggled to keep his emotions under control, sniffling and wiping the moisture from his eyes. "Olivia, Ms. Railey, Tova, and everyone else who is a friend, I wrote this for all of you."

He sat at the piano and performed an original piece that brought tears to everyone's eyes and ended with a raucous applause. Arben was overcome by the response. He stood and bowed, then turned and began clapping, directing the applause to Tova, Ms. Railey, Olivia, the doctors, and the team. "It's not loud," he called out, drawing laughter.

He smiled, sat back down, and played his second set.

As the evening came to an end, Arben chatted with everyone, completely at ease, interacting with people like he never had before.

Epilogue

In the weeks that followed, Arben and Tova were back on the road full-time, performing three to four nights a week, with their calendar quickly filling for months to come.

Due to the discovery of Arben's Vent, Dr. Carver graced the covers of several prominent medical journals. He continued working with Arben as part of the team's ongoing research.

Arben was placed with a skilled therapist to discuss his troubled childhood and a linguist who began the long journey of helping him decipher the voices he heard and the messages he had been receiving all his life. They met regularly, although with Arben frequently traveling, they often met online.

Arben's journey captivated the nation, propelling him into the national spotlight. Tova handled the press while Arben continued to perform to packed rooms. Despite their demanding schedules, they occasionally took time off for Tova to spend time with David and for Arben to meet with the medical community, where he answered questions and discussed his progress.

Public interest reached a point where Arben was invited to be a guest on a national talk show. Sitting across from the interviewer, he was asked how it all began. With a casual shrug, Arben replied, “Nature called.”

ACKNOWLEDGEMENT

A special thanks to Ami Gordon for her editing and input.

Additional thanks to Joelle Yudin for her initial feedback.